ANNOYING ORANGE™

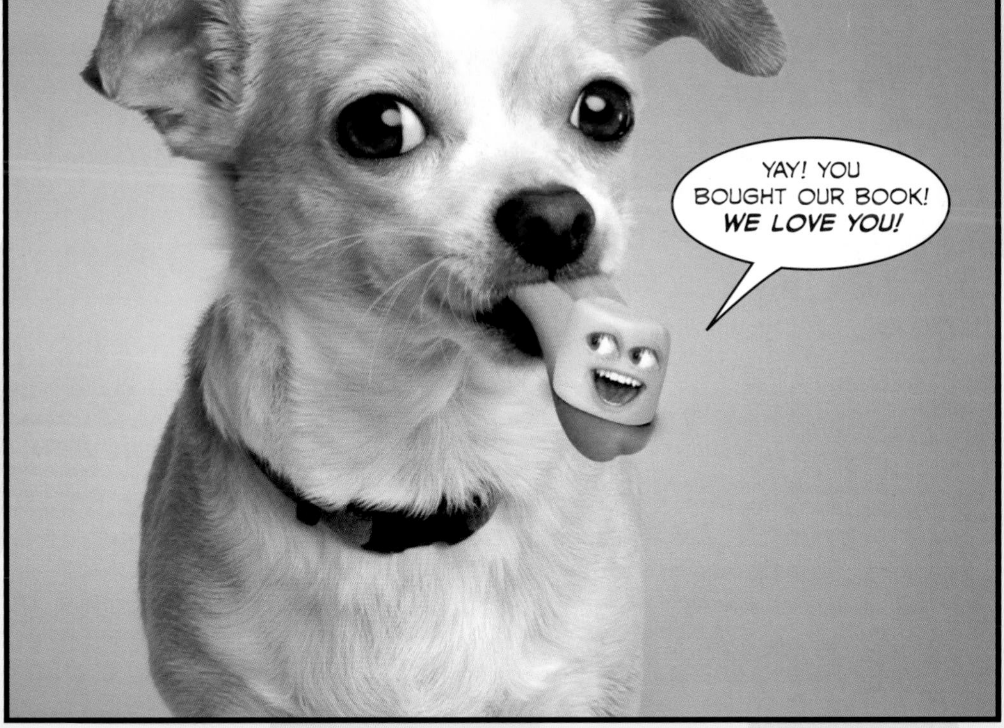
YAY! YOU BOUGHT OUR BOOK! *WE LOVE YOU!*

PAPERCUTZ™

ANNOYING ORANGE

AND OTHER GRAPHIC NOVELS AVAILABLE FROM PAPERCUT**Z**

COMING SOON!

ANNOYING ORANGE
Graphic Novel #1
"Secret Agent
Orange"

ANNOYING ORANGE
Graphic Novel #2
"Orange You Glad
You're Not Me?"

ANNOYING ORANGE
Graphic Novel #3
"Pulped Fiction"

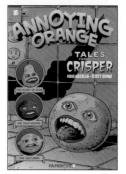

ANNOYING ORANGE
Graphic Novel #4
"Tales from the
Crisper"

PAPERCUTZ
SLICES
Graphic Novel #1
"Harry Potty
and the Deathly
Boring"

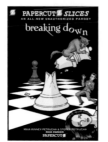

PAPERCUTZ
SLICES
Graphic Novel #2
"breaking down"

PAPERCUTZ
SLICES
Graphic Novel #3
"Percy Jerkson &
The Ovolacto-
vegetarians"

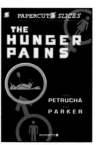

PAPERCUTZ
SLICES
Graphic Novel #4
"The Hunger
Pains"

PAPERCUTZ
SLICES
Graphic Novel #5
"The Farting
Dead"

**ANNOYING ORANGE and PAPERCUTZ SLICES graphic novels,
the print editions, are still available at booksellers everywhere.**

Or order directly from Papercutz. ANNOYING ORANGE and PAPERCUTZ SLICES are available in
paperback for $6.99 each; in hardcover for $10.99, except ANNOYING ORANGE #2, hardcover is
$11.99, and ANNOYING ORANGE #3 and #4 are $7.99 paperback, and $11.99 hardcover. Please add
$4.00 for postage and handling for the first book, and add $1.00 for each additional book.
Make check payable to NBM Publishing.

Send to: Papercutz, 160 Broadway, Suite 700, East Wing, New York, NY 10038

Or call 800-886-1223 between 9-5 EST, M-F. Visa, MC, and AmEx accepted.

www.papercutz.com

ANNOYING ORANGE and PAPERCUTZ SLICES graphic novels
are also available digitally wherever e-books are sold.

PULPED FICTION

WHO THE HECK IS "ANN O. YING" AND HOW DID SHE GET *TOP BILLING?!*

Annoying Orange is created by DANE BOEDIGHEIMER

SCOTT SHAW! – Writer & Artist

MIKE KAZALEH – Writer & Artist

LAURIE E. SMITH – Colorist

PAPERCUTZ™
NEW YORK

#3 "Pulped Fiction"
"Skipping Orange"
"Marshmallow Gets Down With its Peeps"
"The Story of Paul Onion"
"Nerville's Magna Carta"
Mike Kazaleh – Writer & Artist
Laurie E. Smith – Colorist
Tom Orzechowski – Letterer
"The Seed of Crime Fears Better Fruit-- Now with Extra Pulp!"
Scott Shaw! – Writer & Artist
Laurie E. Smith – Colorist
Janice Chiang – Letterer

Special thanks to: Gary Binkow, Tim Blankley, Dane Boedigheimer,
Spencer Grove, Teresa Harris, Reza Izad, Debra Joester, Polina Rey, Tom Sheppard, Grace Wen
Director of Marketing: Jesse Post
Production Coordinator: Beth Scorzato
Associate Editor: Michael Petranek
Jim Salicrup
Editor-in-Chief

ISBN: 978-1-59707-420-9 paperback edition
ISBN: 978-1-59707-421-6 hardcover edition

TM & © 2013 Annoying Orange, Inc.
Used under license by 14th Hour Productions, LLC.
Editorial matter Copyright © 2013 by Papercutz.

Printed in Canada
July 2013 by Friesens Printing
1 Printers Way
Altona, MB ROG OBO

Papercutz books may be purchased for business or promotional use.
For information on bulk purchases please contact Macmillan Corporate
and Premium Sales Department at (800) 221-7945 x5442.

Distributed by Macmillan
First Printing

MEET THE FRUIT...

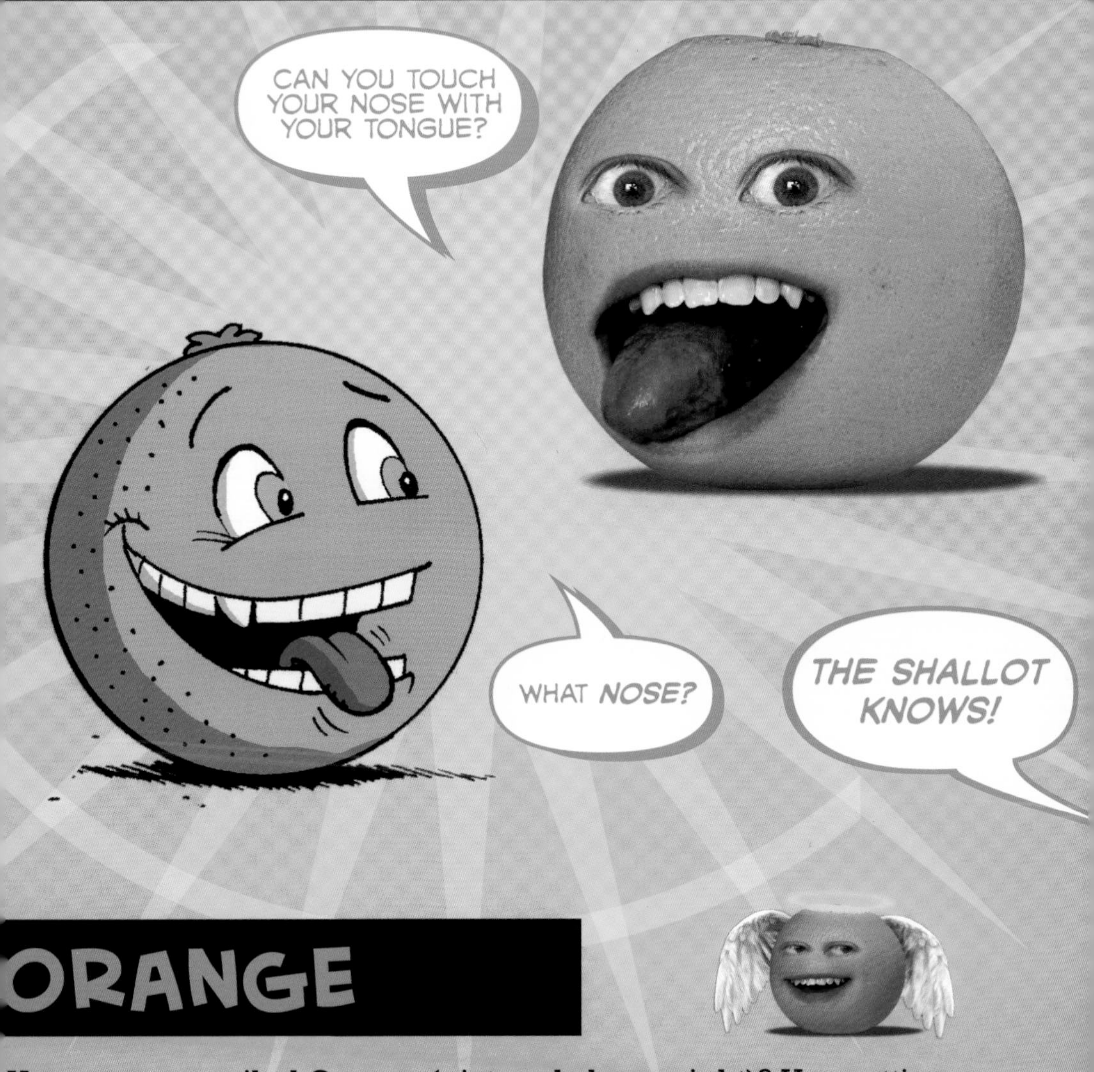
CAN YOU TOUCH YOUR NOSE WITH YOUR TONGUE?
WHAT *NOSE?*
THE SHALLOT KNOWS!

ORANGE

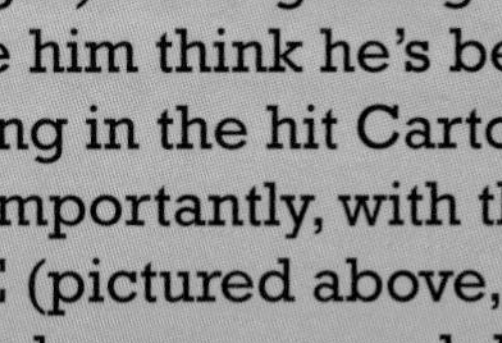

Has success spoiled Orange (pictured above, right)? Has getting over a gazillion hits on his YouTube videos made him think he's better than other fruit, aside from Apple? Has starring in the hit Cartoon Network TV series gone to his head? And most importantly, with the humongous success of the ANNOYING ORANGE (pictured above, left) graphic novel series from Papercutz, has Orange become so celebrated, that his ego now dwarves the ego of every other star in Hollywood combined? Or has he miraculously remained unchanged? Is he still the same cute, sweet (sort of), yet annoying fruit his fans and friends have grown to love? We asked several of his friends for their opinions on this pressing issue...!

PEAR

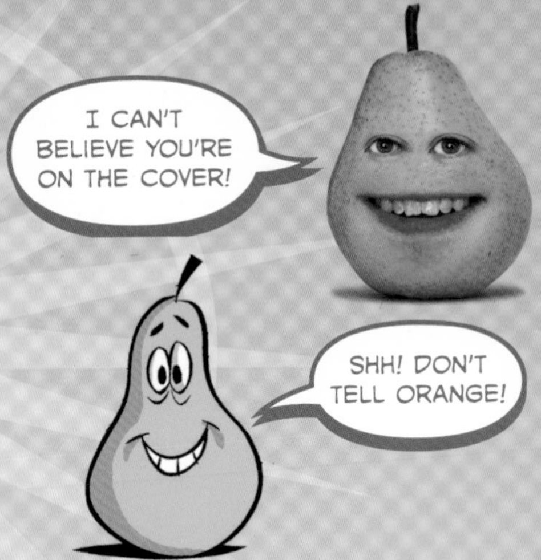
I CAN'T BELIEVE YOU'RE ON THE COVER!
SHH! DON'T TELL ORANGE!

We asked Pear "Has success spoiled Orange?" and after pondering for just a few moments, he slyly evaded the question by answering, "No! Orange is not spoiled at all! Nerville has done an excellent job of making sure each and every fruit at Daneboe's Supermarket is kept as fresh as possible. Orange spoiled? Of course not! He's as fresh as ever—just look at him!" Spoken like the true friend to Orange that Pear is known to be. When we explained that we didn't mean "spoiled" literally, Pear replied, "Well, then I literally don't know what you're talking about."

MIDGET APPLE

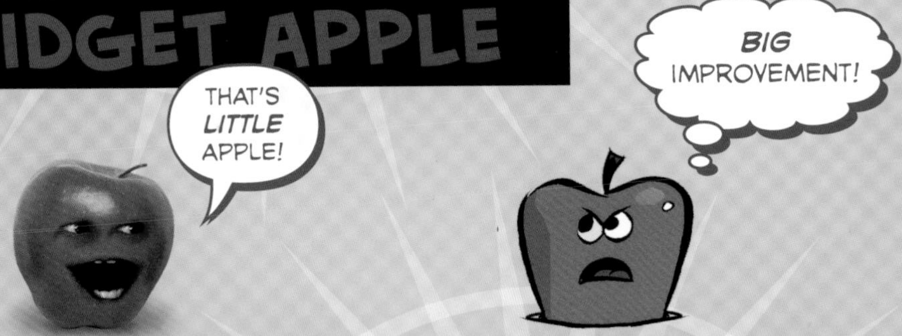
THAT'S *LITTLE* APPLE!
BIG IMPROVEMENT!

When we attempted to ask Midget Apple the same question, we didn't get very far. We started simply by saying, "Excuse us, Midget Apple—" and he quickly cut us off. "My name IS NOT Midget Apple! How many times must I tell everyone that?!" He then stormed off, leaving before we could even finish asking our question.

GRANDPA LEMON

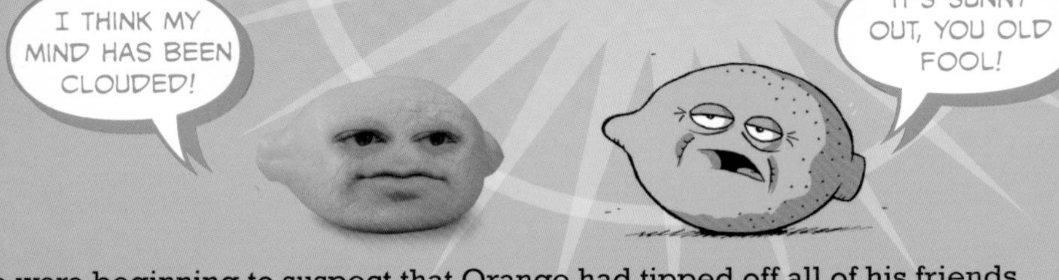
I THINK MY MIND HAS BEEN CLOUDED!
IT'S SUNNY OUT, YOU OLD FOOL!

We were beginning to suspect that Orange had tipped off all of his friends and asked them not to speak to us. Or if they did, not answer our question. For example, we asked Grandpa Lemon if he thought success spoiled Orange, and he replied, "Why would 'recess' spoil him? Everyone loves recess! That's when school's out!" We tried asking again, but before we could finish the question, the old fruit fell fast asleep.

PASSION FRUIT

WE'RE *FRUITILICIOUS!*

Passion Fruit was far more cooperative. When asked if success spoiled Orange, she quickly replied "Of course not! He has always been exactly the way he is—annoying, yet somewhat lovable despite himself. There's something about him that's irresistible, but I can't quite figure out what!"

MARSHMALLOW

I *LOVE* UNICORNS!

ME TOO! *YAY!*

Marshmallow was willing to answer the question "Has success spoiled Orange?" But we're still trying to figure out Marshmallow's answer—"Orange is Orange! And Orange is one of the colors of the rainbow and I love rainbows! Yay! Answering questions is fun!"

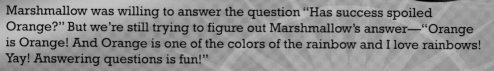

GRAPEFRUIT

IF I WAS ANY MORE PUMPED-UP, I'D *EXPLODE!*

THAT WOULD BE ME *ALL OVER!*

Finally, we asked Grapefruit, "Has success spoiled Orange?" Here's his answer: "What 'success'? Any success that's come that whiny little citrus' way has been due to me! The only reason anyone pays attention to his videos, TV show, or graphic novels is because they're hoping to get a glimpse of me! You know it's true!" With that, we simply gave up.

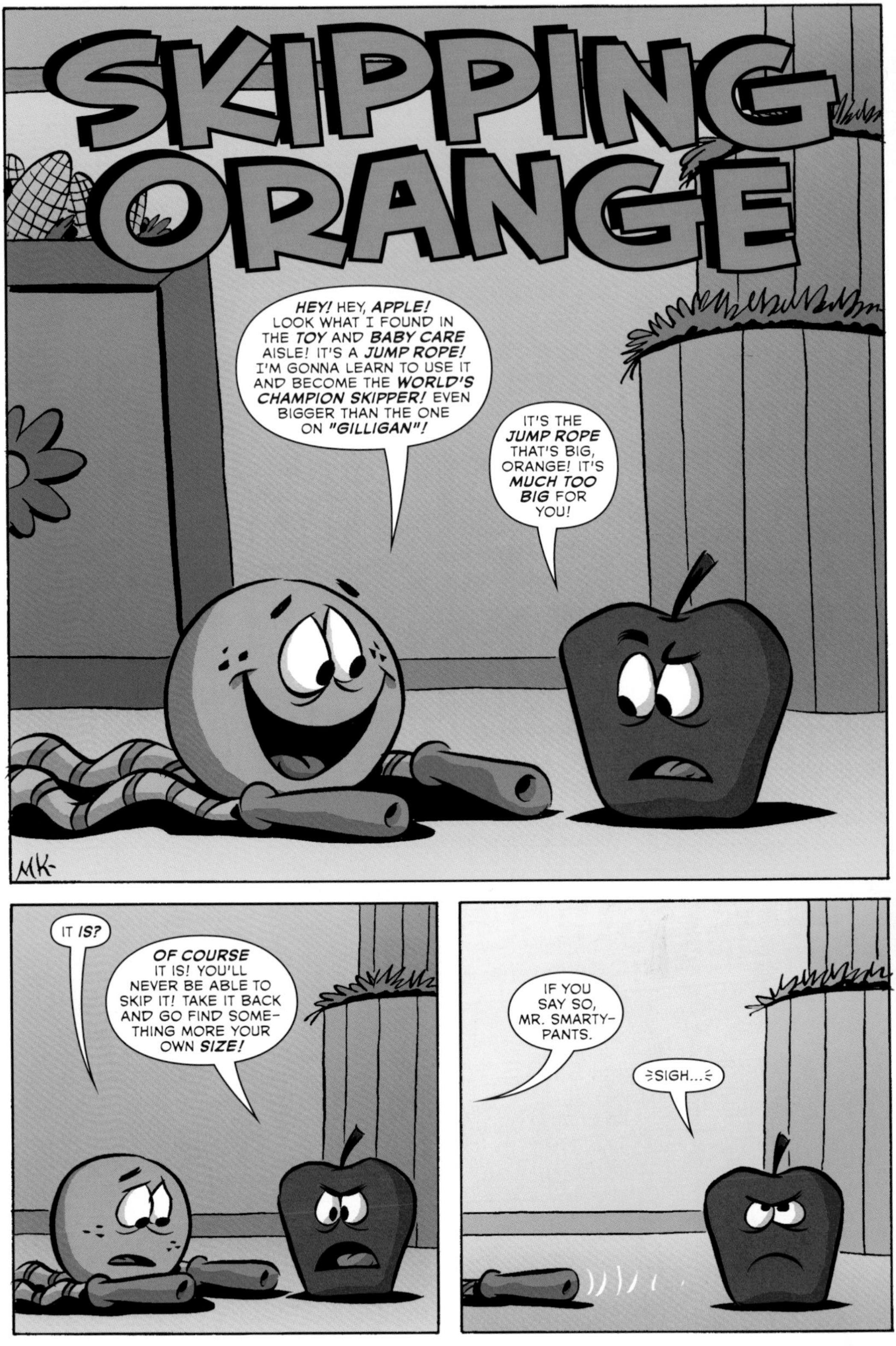
SKIPPING ORANGE
HEY! HEY, APPLE! LOOK WHAT I FOUND IN THE TOY AND BABY CARE AISLE! IT'S A JUMP ROPE! I'M GONNA LEARN TO USE IT AND BECOME THE WORLD'S CHAMPION SKIPPER! EVEN BIGGER THAN THE ONE ON "GILLIGAN"!
IT'S THE JUMP ROPE THAT'S BIG, ORANGE! IT'S MUCH TOO BIG FOR YOU!
MK
IT IS?
OF COURSE IT IS! YOU'LL NEVER BE ABLE TO SKIP IT! TAKE IT BACK AND GO FIND SOME-THING MORE YOUR OWN SIZE!
IF YOU SAY SO, MR. SMARTY-PANTS.
SIGH...

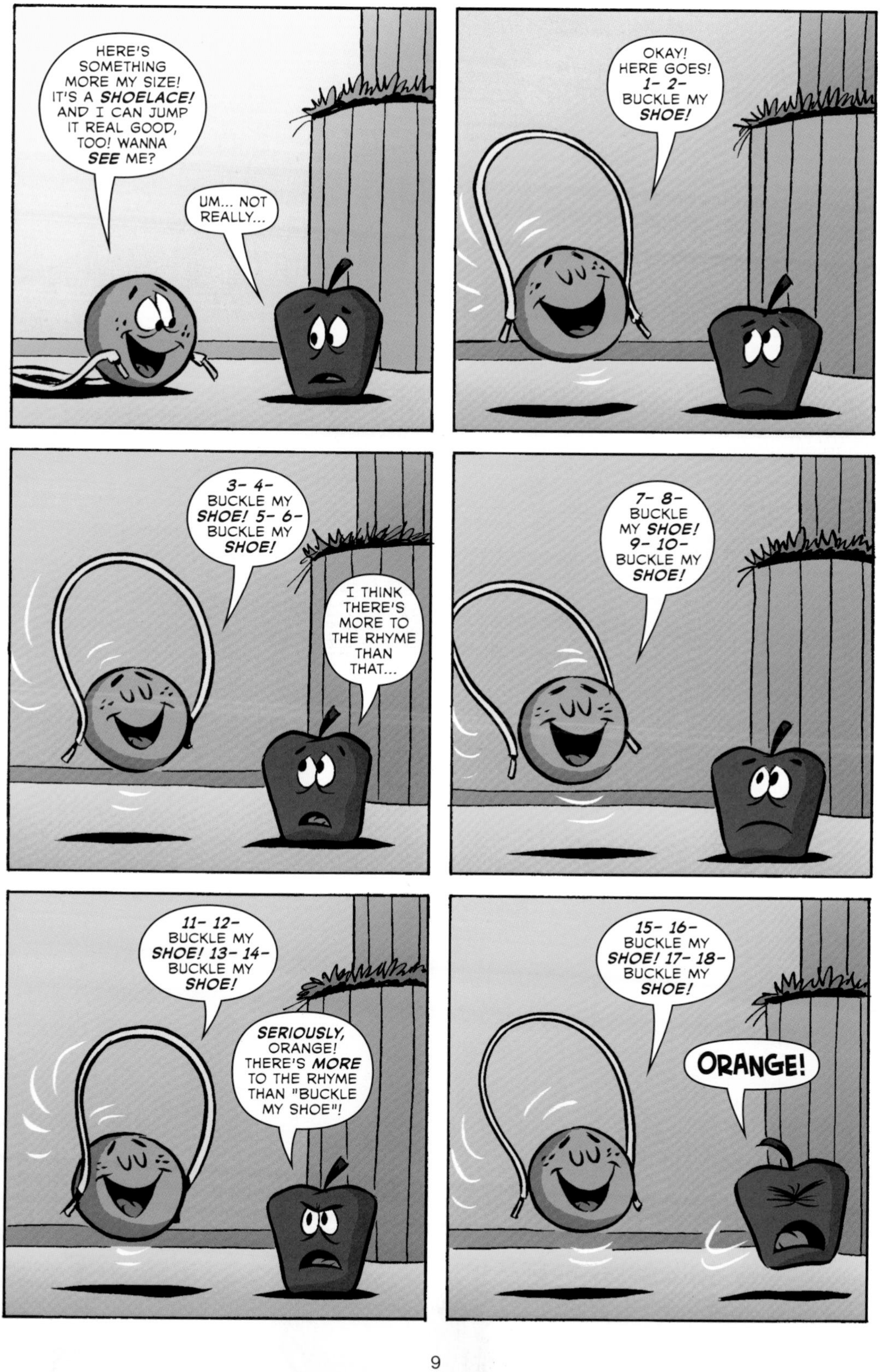
HERE'S SOMETHING MORE MY SIZE! IT'S A **SHOELACE!** AND I CAN JUMP IT REAL GOOD, TOO! WANNA **SEE** ME?
UM... NOT REALLY...
OKAY! HERE GOES! ***1- 2-*** BUCKLE MY ***SHOE!***
3- 4- BUCKLE MY ***SHOE! 5- 6-*** BUCKLE MY ***SHOE!***
I THINK THERE'S MORE TO THE RHYME THAN THAT...
7- 8- BUCKLE MY ***SHOE! 9- 10-*** BUCKLE MY ***SHOE!***
11- 12- BUCKLE MY ***SHOE! 13- 14-*** BUCKLE MY ***SHOE!***
SERIOUSLY, ORANGE! THERE'S ***MORE*** TO THE RHYME THAN "BUCKLE MY SHOE"!
15- 16- BUCKLE MY ***SHOE! 17- 18-*** BUCKLE MY ***SHOE!***
ORANGE!

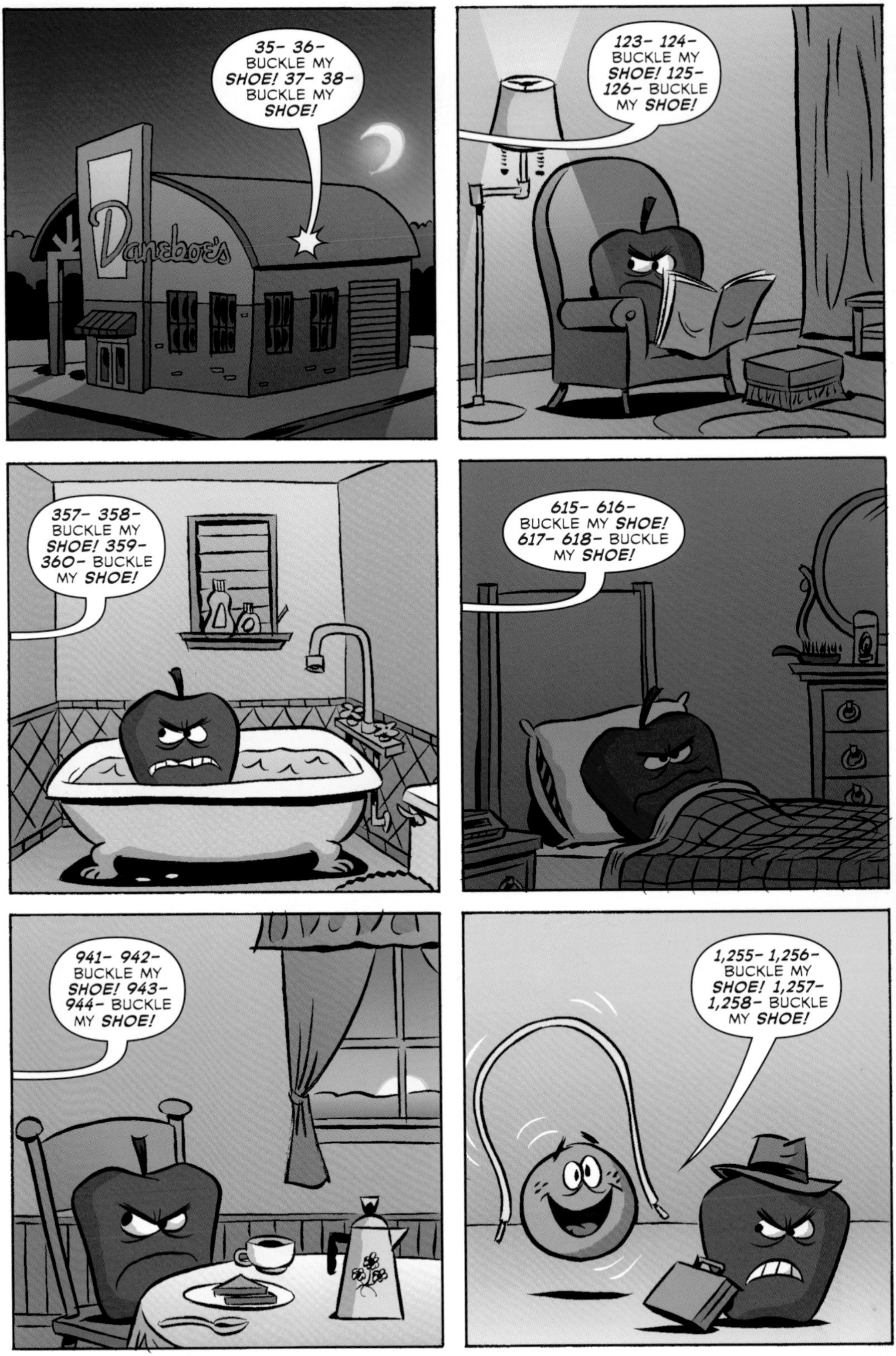
35- 36- BUCKLE MY SHOE! 37- 38- BUCKLE MY SHOE!
Danebore's
123- 124- BUCKLE MY SHOE! 125- 126- BUCKLE MY SHOE!
357- 358- BUCKLE MY SHOE! 359- 360- BUCKLE MY SHOE!
615- 616- BUCKLE MY SHOE! 617- 618- BUCKLE MY SHOE!
941- 942- BUCKLE MY SHOE! 943- 944- BUCKLE MY SHOE!
1,255- 1,256- BUCKLE MY SHOE! 1,257- 1,258- BUCKLE MY SHOE!

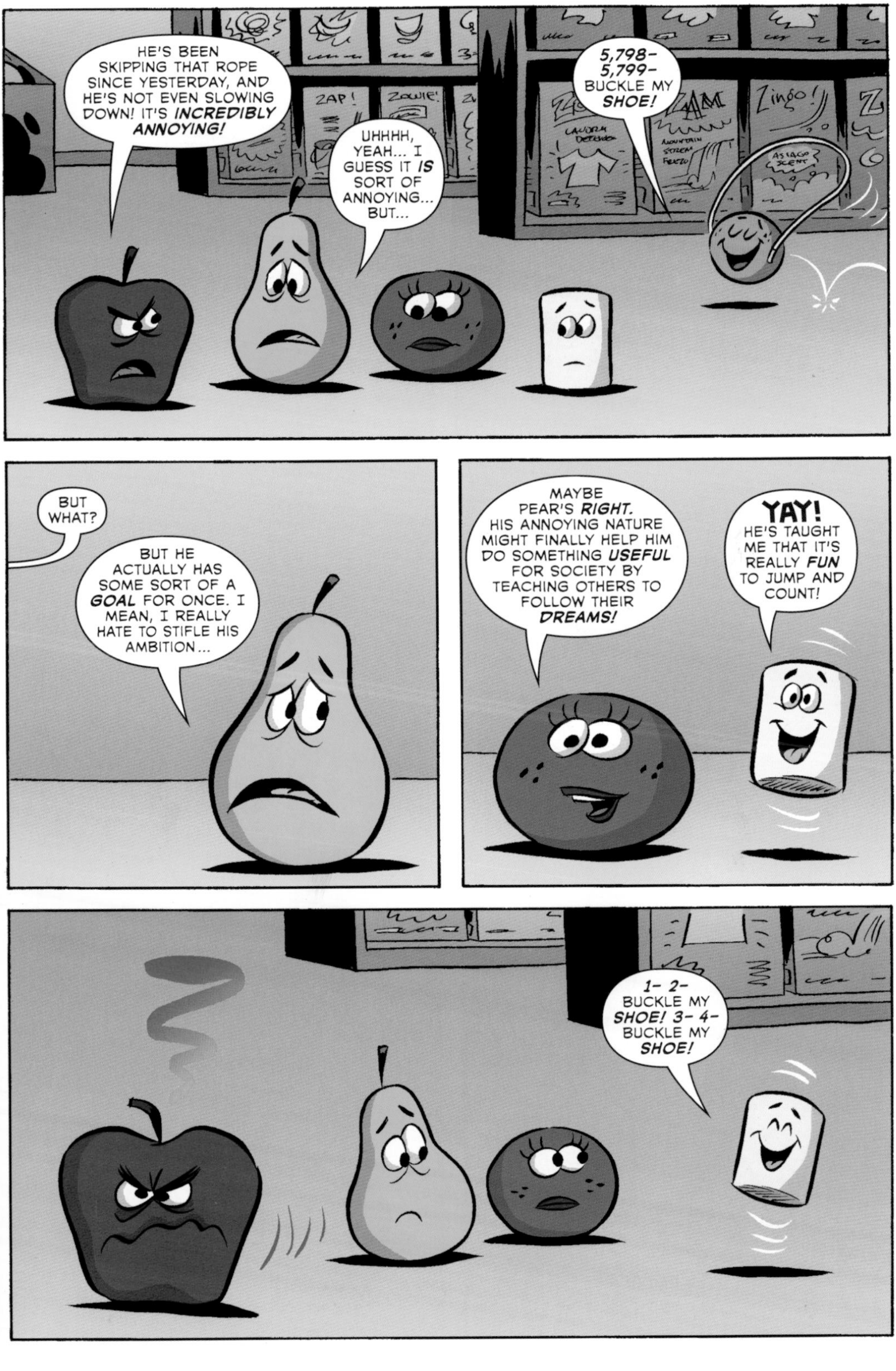

HE'S BEEN SKIPPING THAT ROPE SINCE YESTERDAY, AND HE'S NOT EVEN SLOWING DOWN! IT'S *INCREDIBLY ANNOYING!*
UHHHH, YEAH... I GUESS IT *IS* SORT OF ANNOYING... BUT...
5,798– 5,799– BUCKLE MY *SHOE!*
BUT WHAT?
BUT HE ACTUALLY HAS SOME SORT OF A *GOAL* FOR ONCE. I MEAN, I REALLY HATE TO STIFLE HIS AMBITION...
MAYBE PEAR'S *RIGHT.* HIS ANNOYING NATURE MIGHT FINALLY HELP HIM DO SOMETHING *USEFUL* FOR SOCIETY BY TEACHING OTHERS TO FOLLOW THEIR *DREAMS!*
YAY! HE'S TAUGHT ME THAT IT'S REALLY *FUN* TO JUMP AND COUNT!
1– 2– BUCKLE MY *SHOE! 3– 4–* BUCKLE MY *SHOE!*

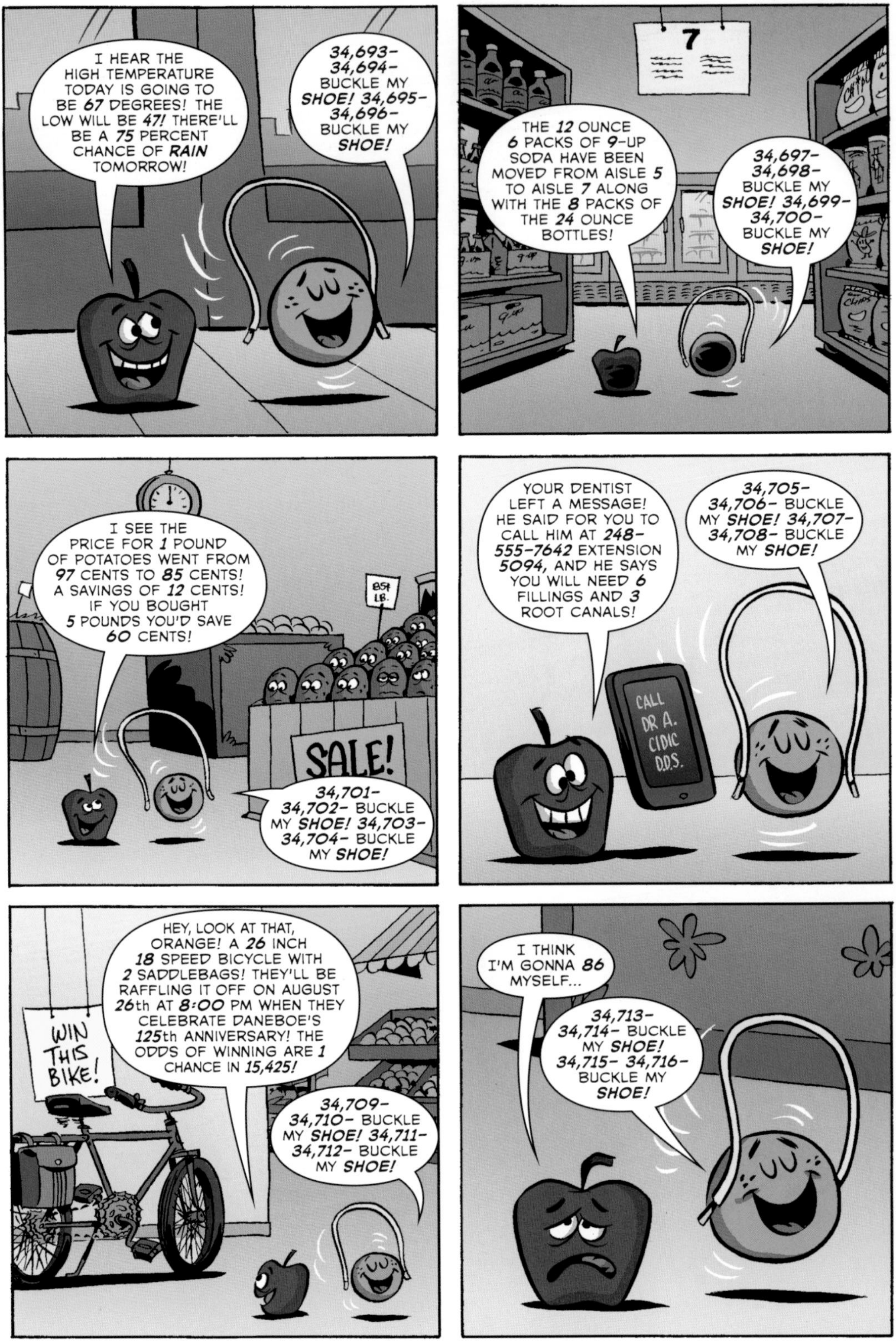
I HEAR THE HIGH TEMPERATURE TODAY IS GOING TO BE 67 DEGREES! THE LOW WILL BE 47! THERE'LL BE A 75 PERCENT CHANCE OF RAIN TOMORROW!
34,693- 34,694- BUCKLE MY SHOE! 34,695- 34,696- BUCKLE MY SHOE!
7
THE 12 OUNCE 6 PACKS OF 9-UP SODA HAVE BEEN MOVED FROM AISLE 5 TO AISLE 7 ALONG WITH THE 8 PACKS OF THE 24 OUNCE BOTTLES!
34,697- 34,698- BUCKLE MY SHOE! 34,699- 34,700- BUCKLE MY SHOE!
I SEE THE PRICE FOR 1 POUND OF POTATOES WENT FROM 97 CENTS TO 85 CENTS! A SAVINGS OF 12 CENTS! IF YOU BOUGHT 5 POUNDS YOU'D SAVE 60 CENTS!
SALE!
34,701- 34,702- BUCKLE MY SHOE! 34,703- 34,704- BUCKLE MY SHOE!
YOUR DENTIST LEFT A MESSAGE! HE SAID FOR YOU TO CALL HIM AT 248-555-7642 EXTENSION 5094, AND HE SAYS YOU WILL NEED 6 FILLINGS AND 3 ROOT CANALS!
34,705- 34,706- BUCKLE MY SHOE! 34,707- 34,708- BUCKLE MY SHOE!
CALL DR A. CIDIC D.D.S.
HEY, LOOK AT THAT, ORANGE! A 26 INCH 18 SPEED BICYCLE WITH 2 SADDLEBAGS! THEY'LL BE RAFFLING IT OFF ON AUGUST 26th AT 8:00 PM WHEN THEY CELEBRATE DANEBOE'S 125th ANNIVERSARY! THE ODDS OF WINNING ARE 1 CHANCE IN 15,425!
WIN THIS BIKE!
34,709- 34,710- BUCKLE MY SHOE! 34,711- 34,712- BUCKLE MY SHOE!
I THINK I'M GONNA 86 MYSELF...
34,713- 34,714- BUCKLE MY SHOE! 34,715- 34,716- BUCKLE MY SHOE!

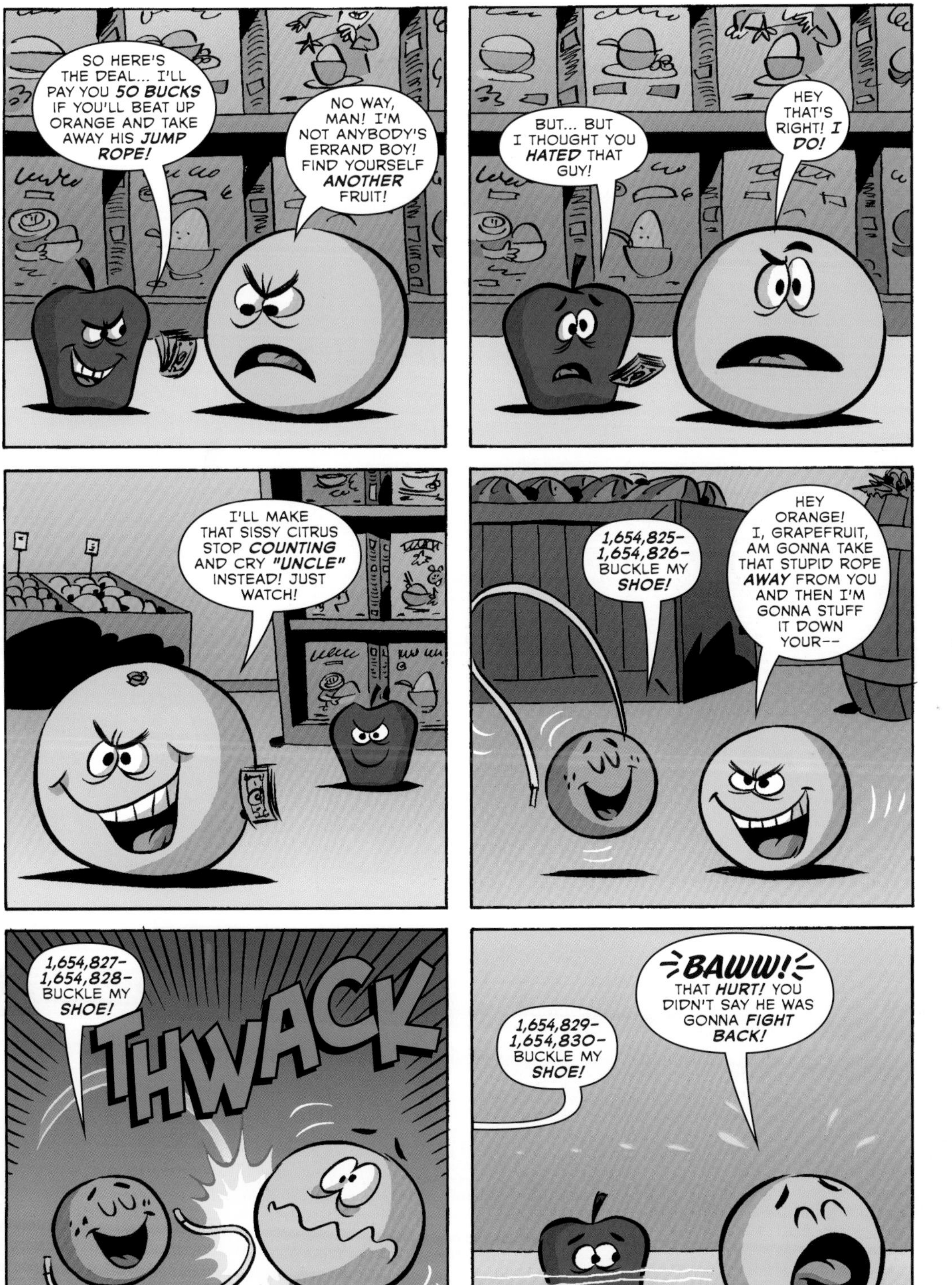
SO HERE'S THE DEAL... I'LL PAY YOU 50 BUCKS IF YOU'LL BEAT UP ORANGE AND TAKE AWAY HIS JUMP ROPE!
NO WAY, MAN! I'M NOT ANYBODY'S ERRAND BOY! FIND YOURSELF ANOTHER FRUIT!
BUT... BUT I THOUGHT YOU HATED THAT GUY!
HEY THAT'S RIGHT! I DO!
I'LL MAKE THAT SISSY CITRUS STOP COUNTING AND CRY "UNCLE" INSTEAD! JUST WATCH!
1,654,825- 1,654,826- BUCKLE MY SHOE!
HEY ORANGE! I, GRAPEFRUIT, AM GONNA TAKE THAT STUPID ROPE AWAY FROM YOU AND THEN I'M GONNA STUFF IT DOWN YOUR--
1,654,827- 1,654,828- BUCKLE MY SHOE!
THWACK
1,654,829- 1,654,830- BUCKLE MY SHOE!
BAWW! THAT HURT! YOU DIDN'T SAY HE WAS GONNA FIGHT BACK!

ISN'T THERE SOMETHING YOU CAN *DO* ABOUT THIS, NERVILLE? THAT *SKIPPING* AND *COUNTING* WILL DRIVE US ALL *NUTS* IF IT DOESN'T STOP *SOON!*
OH, I DON'T KNOW, APPLE...
...I MEAN, A LITTLE EXERCISE NEVER HURT *ANYONE!*
BOY, I SURE HOPE THIS THING DOESN'T SPREAD ANY *FURTHER!* IF IT DOES, I'M LIABLE TO...
...TO... T-TO...
1- 2- BUCKLE MY *SHOE!*
3- 4- BUCKLE MY *SHOE!*
5- 6- BUCKLE MY *SHOE!*

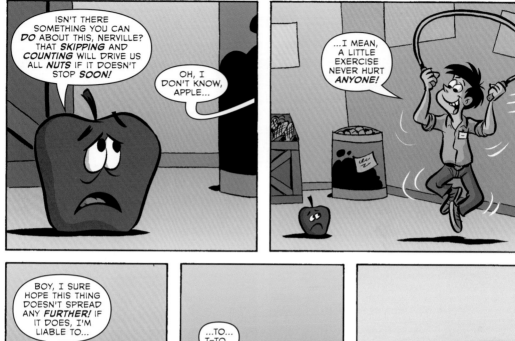

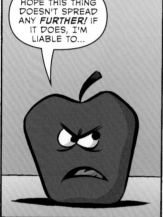

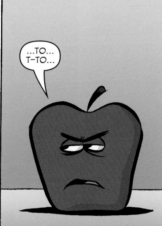

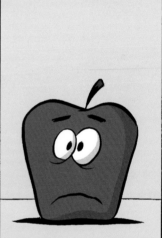

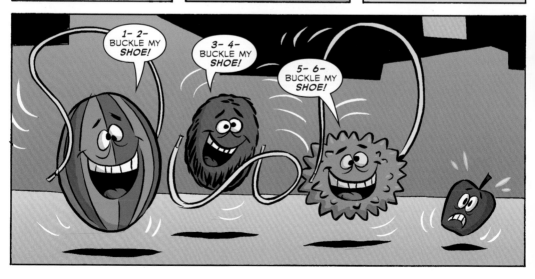

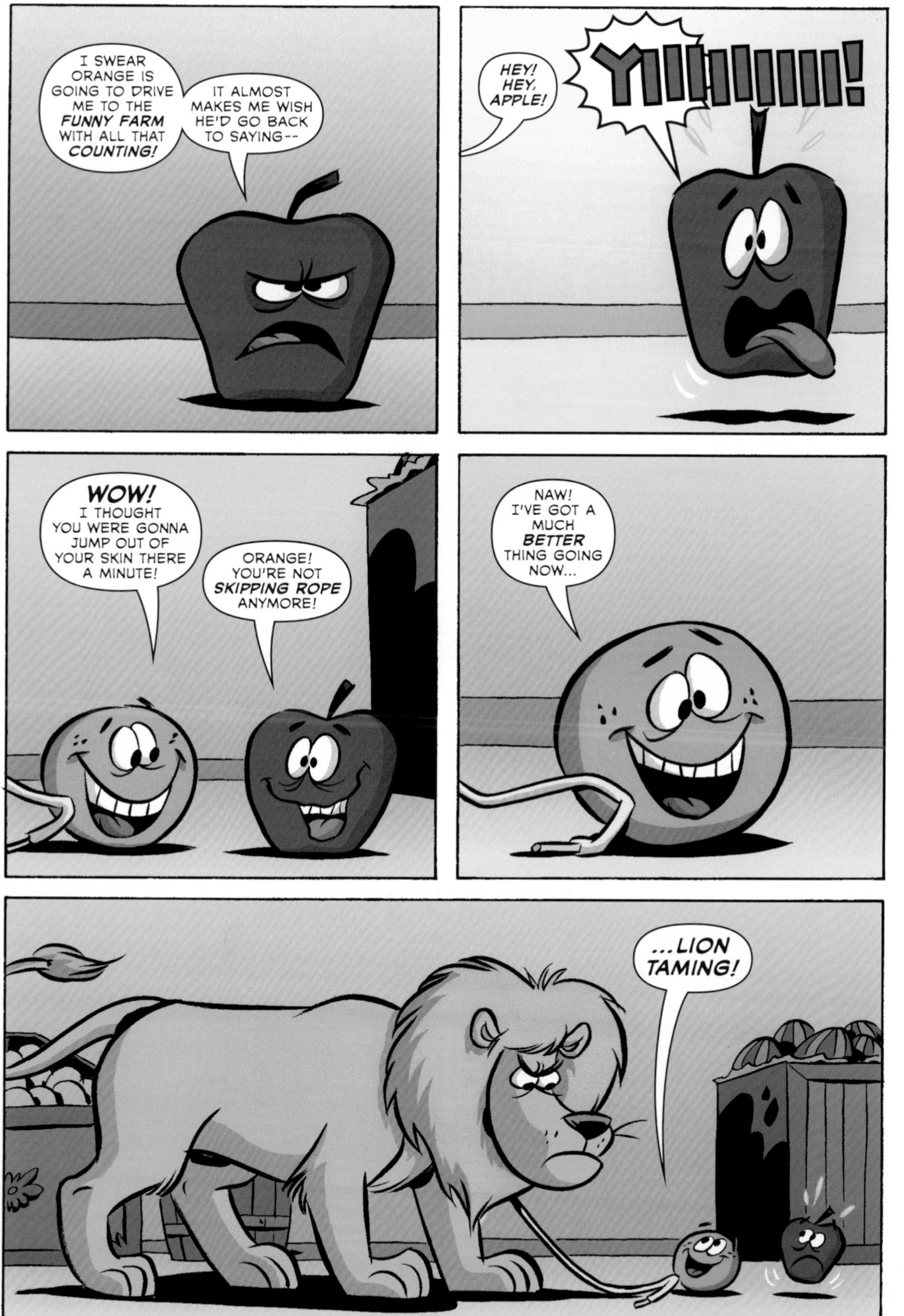
I SWEAR ORANGE IS GOING TO DRIVE ME TO THE FUNNY FARM WITH ALL THAT COUNTING!
IT ALMOST MAKES ME WISH HE'D GO BACK TO SAYING--
HEY! HEY, APPLE!
YIIIIIIIII!
WOW! I THOUGHT YOU WERE GONNA JUMP OUT OF YOUR SKIN THERE A MINUTE!
ORANGE! YOU'RE NOT SKIPPING ROPE ANYMORE!
NAW! I'VE GOT A MUCH BETTER THING GOING NOW...
...LION TAMING!

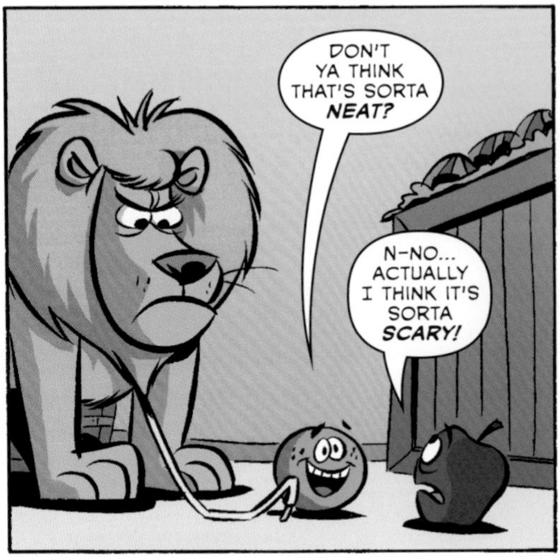
DON'T YA THINK THAT'S SORTA **NEAT?**
N-NO... ACTUALLY I THINK IT'S SORTA **SCARY!**

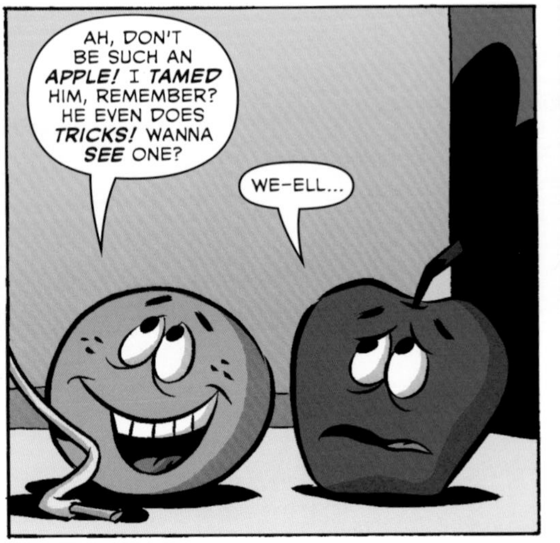
AH, DON'T BE SUCH AN **APPLE!** I **TAMED** HIM, REMEMBER? HE EVEN DOES **TRICKS!** WANNA **SEE** ONE?
WE-ELL...

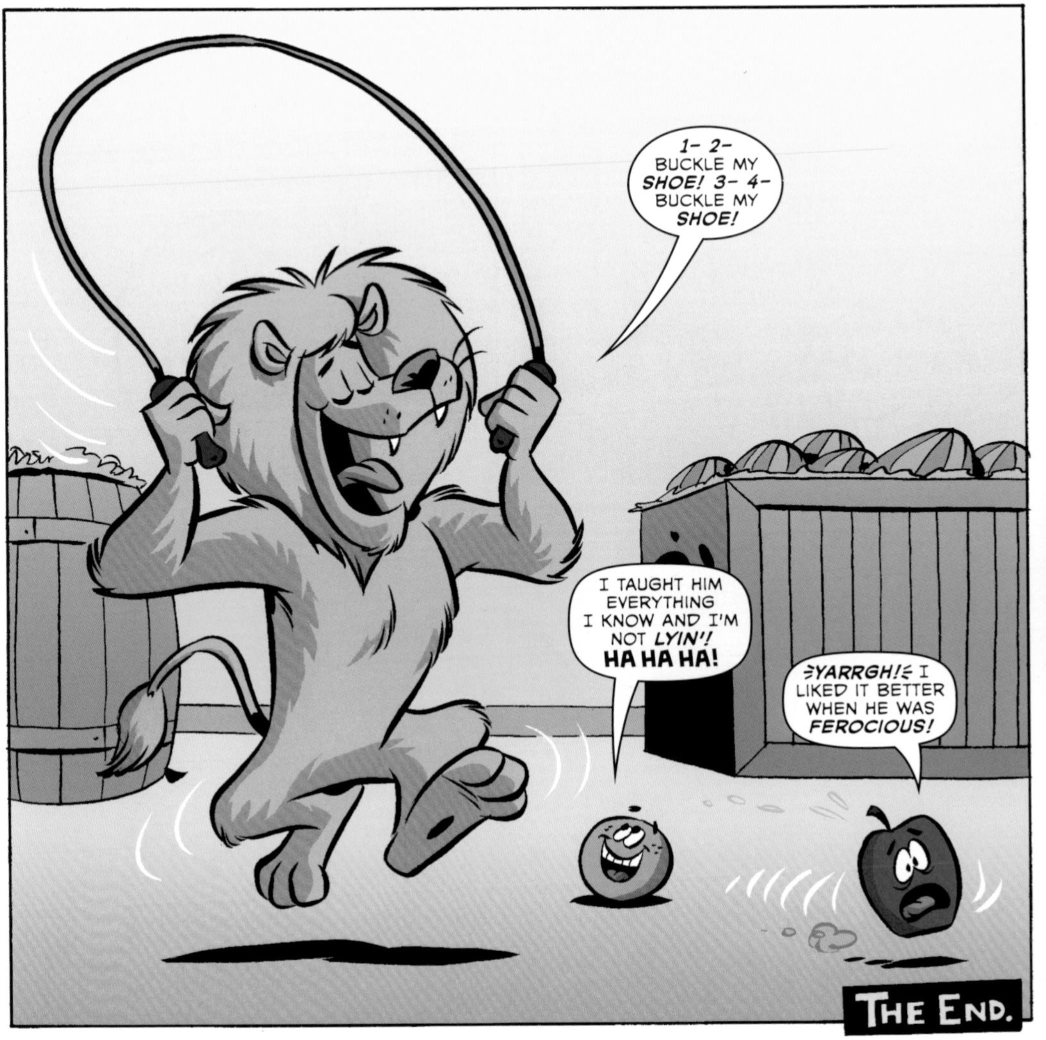
1- 2- BUCKLE MY ***SHOE! 3- 4-*** BUCKLE MY ***SHOE!***
I TAUGHT HIM EVERYTHING I KNOW AND I'M NOT ***LYIN'!*** **HA HA HA!**
YARRGH! I LIKED IT BETTER WHEN HE WAS ***FEROCIOUS!***
THE END.

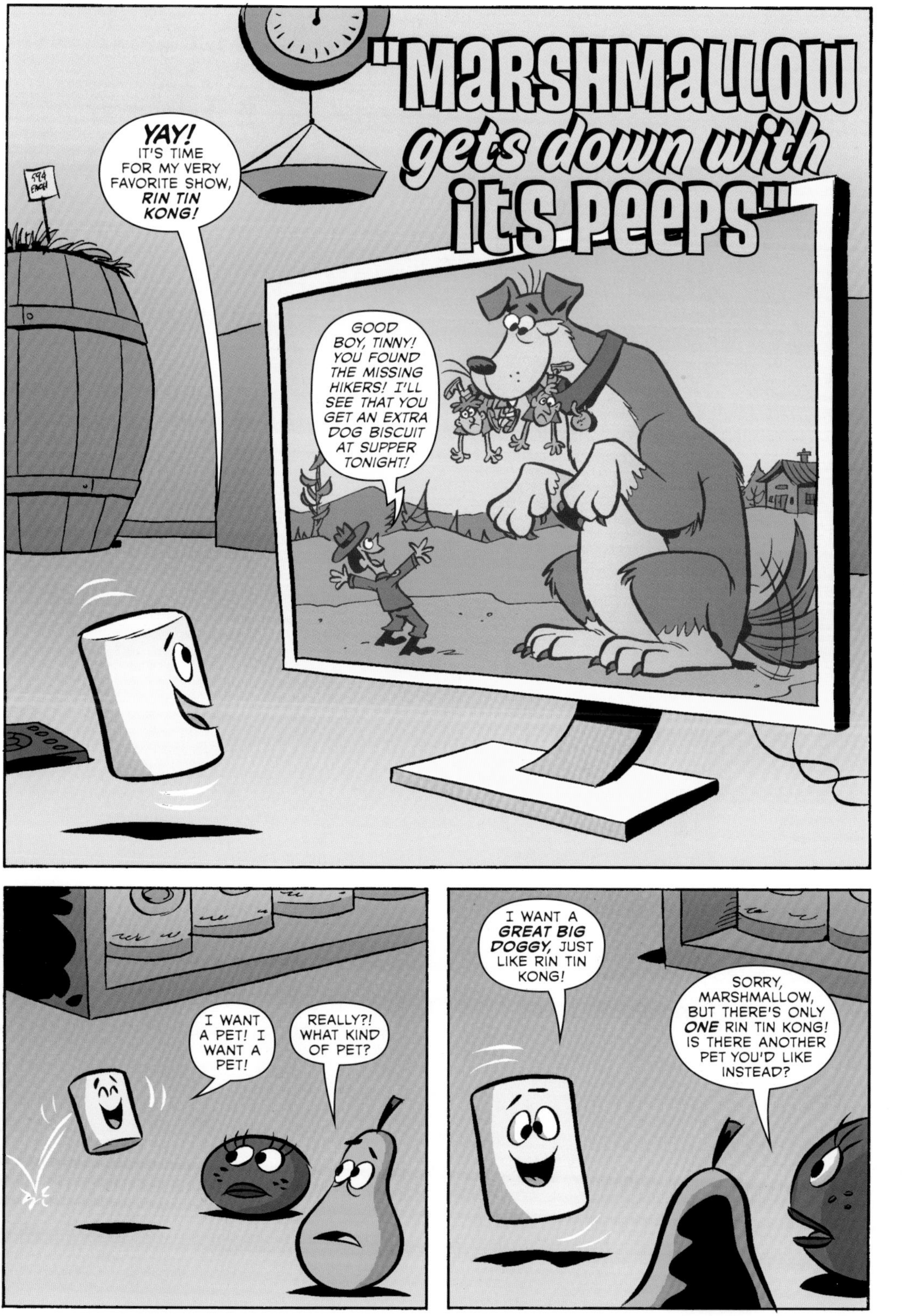
"MARSHMALLOW gets down with its PEEPS"
YAY! IT'S TIME FOR MY VERY FAVORITE SHOW, RIN TIN KONG!
GOOD BOY, TINNY! YOU FOUND THE MISSING HIKERS! I'LL SEE THAT YOU GET AN EXTRA DOG BISCUIT AT SUPPER TONIGHT!
I WANT A PET! I WANT A PET!
REALLY?! WHAT KIND OF PET?
I WANT A GREAT BIG DOGGY, JUST LIKE RIN TIN KONG!
SORRY, MARSHMALLOW, BUT THERE'S ONLY ONE RIN TIN KONG! IS THERE ANOTHER PET YOU'D LIKE INSTEAD?

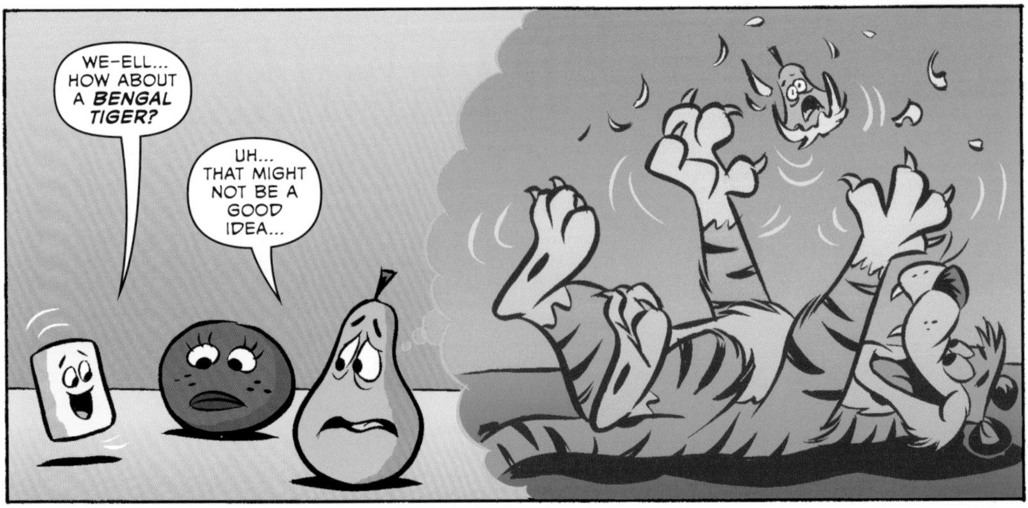
WE-ELL... HOW ABOUT A BENGAL TIGER?
UH... THAT MIGHT NOT BE A GOOD IDEA...

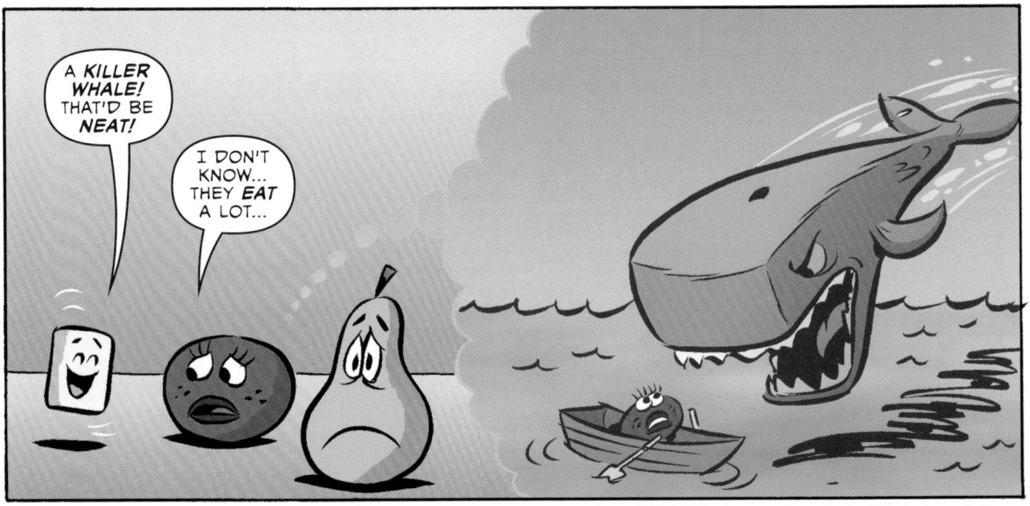
A KILLER WHALE! THAT'D BE NEAT!
I DON'T KNOW... THEY EAT A LOT...

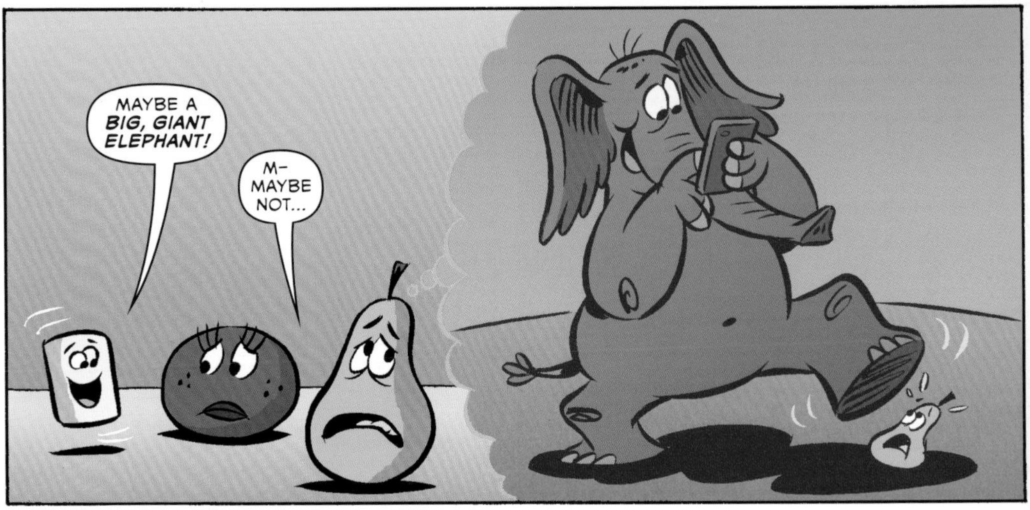
MAYBE A BIG, GIANT ELEPHANT!
M-MAYBE NOT...

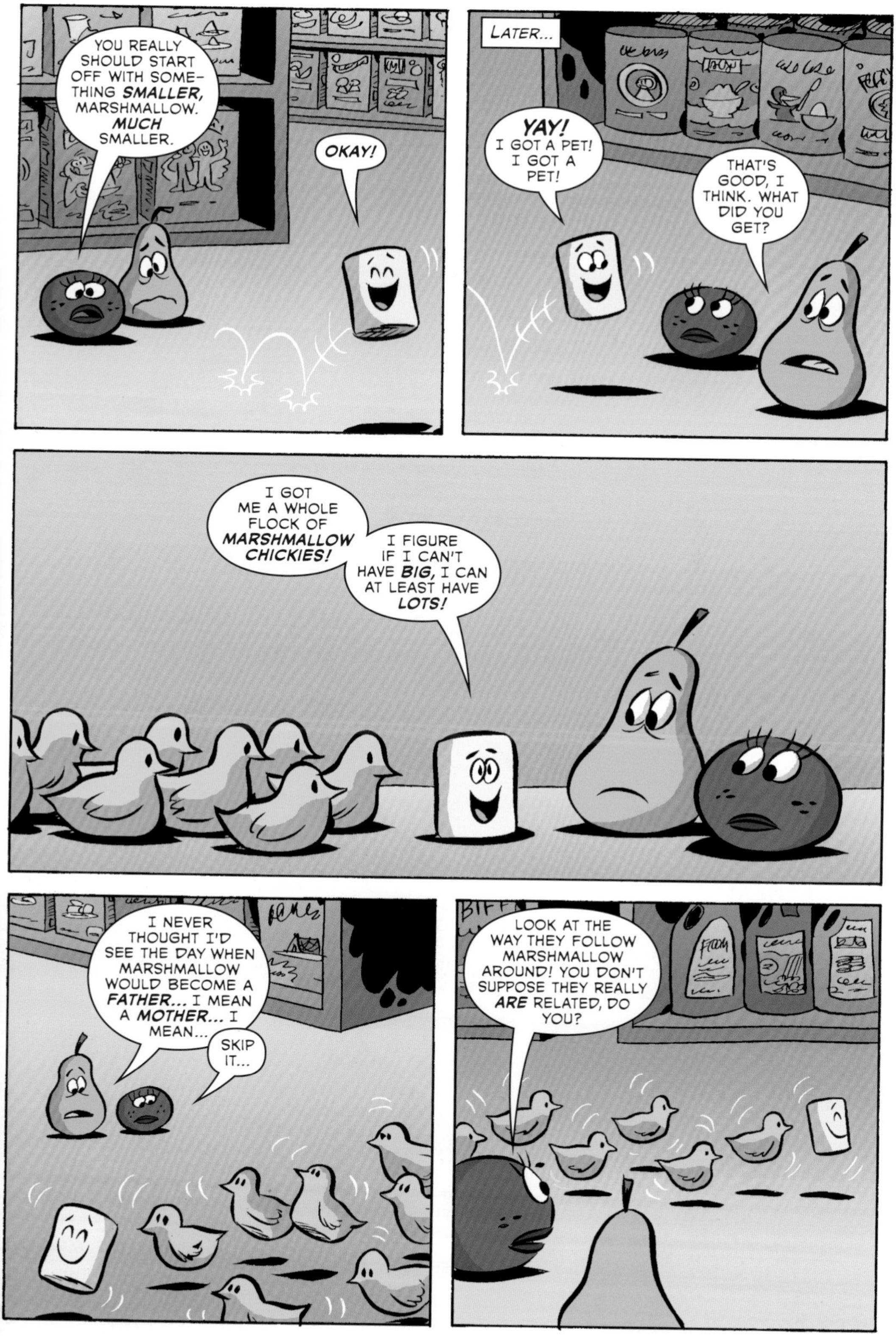
YOU REALLY SHOULD START OFF WITH SOME-THING SMALLER, MARSHMALLOW. MUCH SMALLER.
OKAY!
LATER...
YAY! I GOT A PET! I GOT A PET!
THAT'S GOOD, I THINK. WHAT DID YOU GET?
I GOT ME A WHOLE FLOCK OF MARSHMALLOW CHICKIES!
I FIGURE IF I CAN'T HAVE BIG, I CAN AT LEAST HAVE LOTS!
I NEVER THOUGHT I'D SEE THE DAY WHEN MARSHMALLOW WOULD BECOME A FATHER... I MEAN A MOTHER... I MEAN...
SKIP IT...
LOOK AT THE WAY THEY FOLLOW MARSHMALLOW AROUND! YOU DON'T SUPPOSE THEY REALLY ARE RELATED, DO YOU?

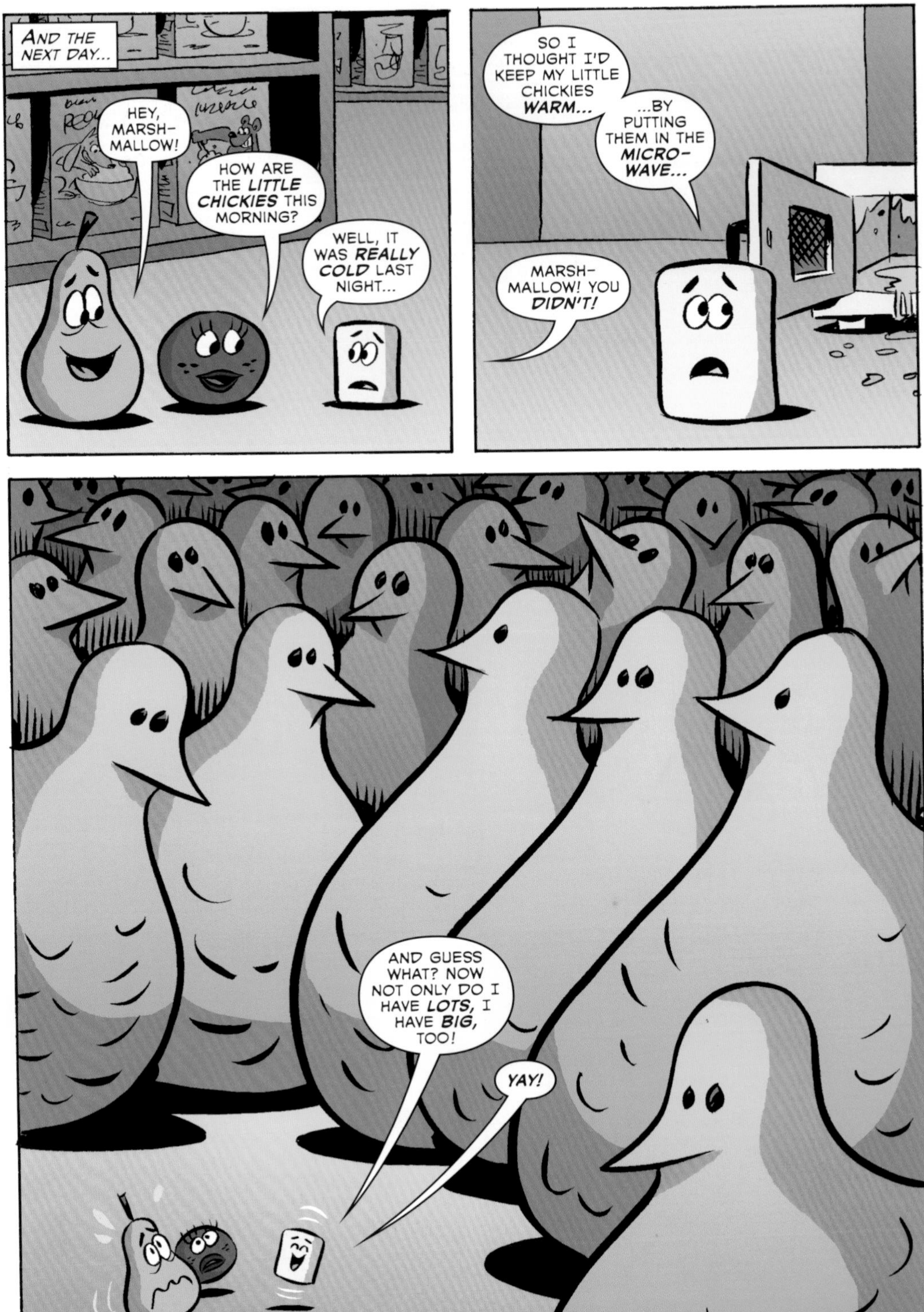
AND THE NEXT DAY...
HEY, MARSH-MALLOW!
HOW ARE THE LITTLE CHICKIES THIS MORNING?
WELL, IT WAS REALLY COLD LAST NIGHT...
SO I THOUGHT I'D KEEP MY LITTLE CHICKIES WARM...
...BY PUTTING THEM IN THE MICRO-WAVE...
MARSH-MALLOW! YOU DIDN'T!
AND GUESS WHAT? NOW NOT ONLY DO I HAVE LOTS, I HAVE BIG, TOO!
YAY!
END.

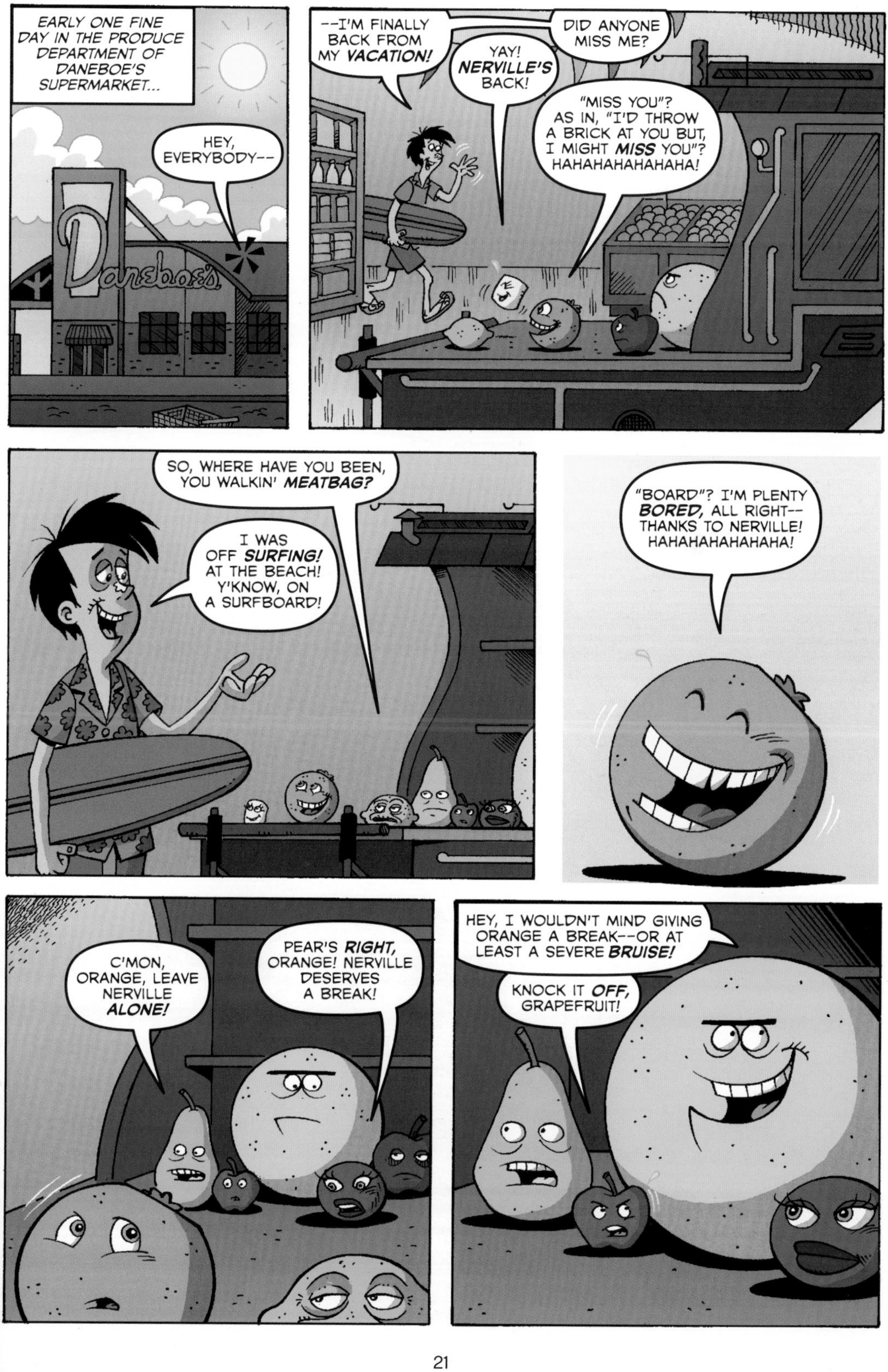
EARLY ONE FINE DAY IN THE PRODUCE DEPARTMENT OF DANEBOE'S SUPERMARKET...
Daneboe's
HEY, EVERYBODY--
--I'M FINALLY BACK FROM MY VACATION!
DID ANYONE MISS ME?
YAY! NERVILLE'S BACK!
"MISS YOU"? AS IN, "I'D THROW A BRICK AT YOU BUT, I MIGHT MISS YOU"? HAHAHAHAHAHAHA!
SO, WHERE HAVE YOU BEEN, YOU WALKIN' MEATBAG?
I WAS OFF SURFING! AT THE BEACH! Y'KNOW, ON A SURFBOARD!
"BOARD"? I'M PLENTY BORED, ALL RIGHT-- THANKS TO NERVILLE! HAHAHAHAHAHAHA!
C'MON, ORANGE, LEAVE NERVILLE ALONE!
PEAR'S RIGHT, ORANGE! NERVILLE DESERVES A BREAK!
HEY, I WOULDN'T MIND GIVING ORANGE A BREAK--OR AT LEAST A SEVERE BRUISE!
KNOCK IT OFF, GRAPEFRUIT!

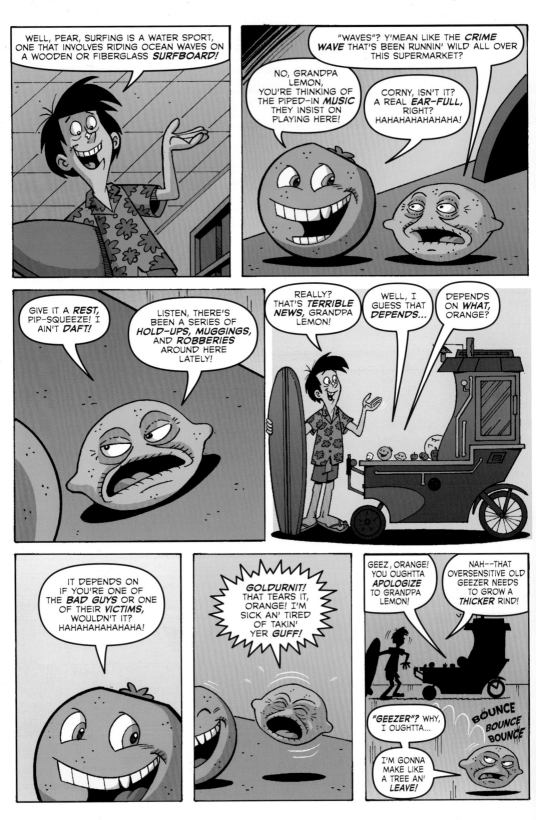

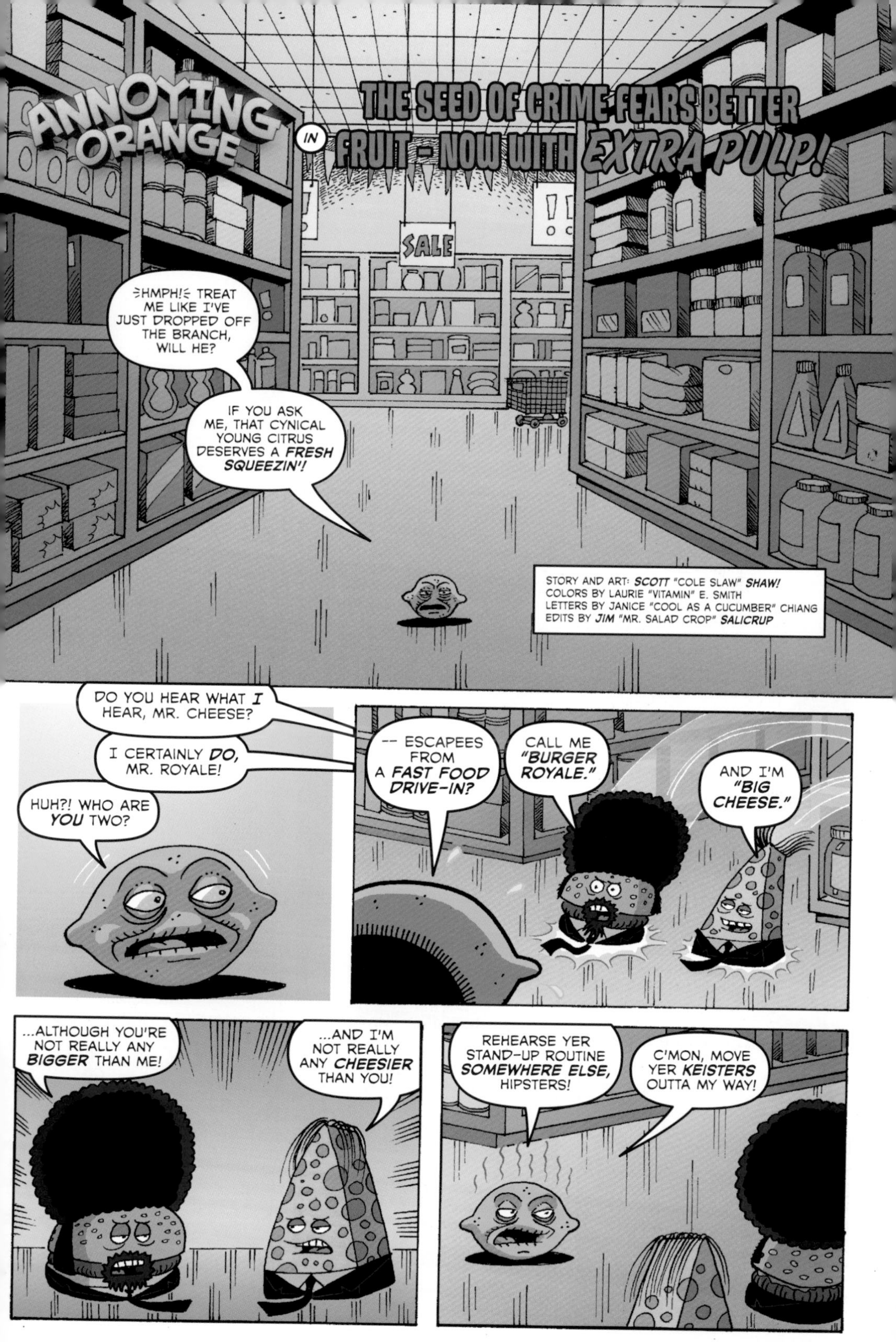
ANNOYING ORANGE
IN
THE SEED OF CRIME FEARS BETTER FRUIT - NOW WITH EXTRA PULP!
SALE
HMPH! TREAT ME LIKE I'VE JUST DROPPED OFF THE BRANCH, WILL HE?
IF YOU ASK ME, THAT CYNICAL YOUNG CITRUS DESERVES A FRESH SQUEEZIN'!
STORY AND ART: SCOTT "COLE SLAW" SHAW!
COLORS BY LAURIE "VITAMIN" E. SMITH
LETTERS BY JANICE "COOL AS A CUCUMBER" CHIANG
EDITS BY JIM "MR. SALAD CROP" SALICRUP
DO YOU HEAR WHAT I HEAR, MR. CHEESE?
I CERTAINLY DO, MR. ROYALE!
HUH?! WHO ARE YOU TWO?
-- ESCAPEES FROM A FAST FOOD DRIVE-IN?
CALL ME "BURGER ROYALE."
AND I'M "BIG CHEESE."
...ALTHOUGH YOU'RE NOT REALLY ANY BIGGER THAN ME!
...AND I'M NOT REALLY ANY CHEESIER THAN YOU!
REHEARSE YER STAND-UP ROUTINE SOMEWHERE ELSE, HIPSTERS!
C'MON, MOVE YER KEISTERS OUTTA MY WAY!

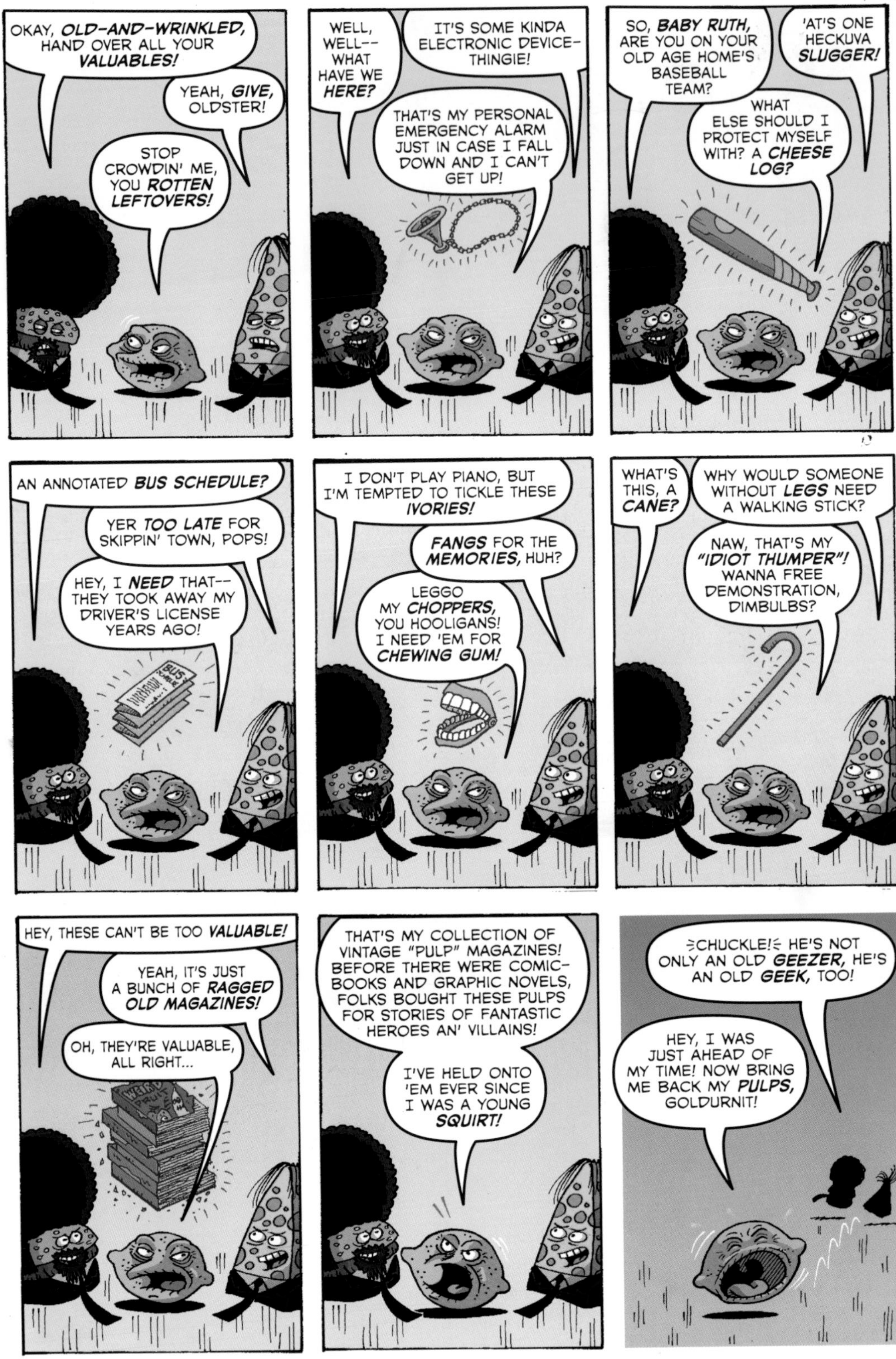
OKAY, OLD-AND-WRINKLED, HAND OVER ALL YOUR VALUABLES!
YEAH, GIVE, OLDSTER!
STOP CROWDIN' ME, YOU ROTTEN LEFTOVERS!
WELL, WELL-- WHAT HAVE WE HERE?
IT'S SOME KINDA ELECTRONIC DEVICE-THINGIE!
THAT'S MY PERSONAL EMERGENCY ALARM JUST IN CASE I FALL DOWN AND I CAN'T GET UP!
SO, BABY RUTH, ARE YOU ON YOUR OLD AGE HOME'S BASEBALL TEAM?
'AT'S ONE HECKUVA SLUGGER!
WHAT ELSE SHOULD I PROTECT MYSELF WITH? A CHEESE LOG?
AN ANNOTATED BUS SCHEDULE?
YER TOO LATE FOR SKIPPIN' TOWN, POPS!
HEY, I NEED THAT-- THEY TOOK AWAY MY DRIVER'S LICENSE YEARS AGO!
I DON'T PLAY PIANO, BUT I'M TEMPTED TO TICKLE THESE IVORIES!
FANGS FOR THE MEMORIES, HUH?
LEGGO MY CHOPPERS, YOU HOOLIGANS! I NEED 'EM FOR CHEWING GUM!
WHAT'S THIS, A CANE?
WHY WOULD SOMEONE WITHOUT LEGS NEED A WALKING STICK?
NAW, THAT'S MY "IDIOT THUMPER"! WANNA FREE DEMONSTRATION, DIMBULBS?
HEY, THESE CAN'T BE TOO VALUABLE!
YEAH, IT'S JUST A BUNCH OF RAGGED OLD MAGAZINES!
OH, THEY'RE VALUABLE, ALL RIGHT...
THAT'S MY COLLECTION OF VINTAGE "PULP" MAGAZINES! BEFORE THERE WERE COMIC-BOOKS AND GRAPHIC NOVELS, FOLKS BOUGHT THESE PULPS FOR STORIES OF FANTASTIC HEROES AN' VILLAINS!
I'VE HELD ONTO 'EM EVER SINCE I WAS A YOUNG SQUIRT!
CHUCKLE! HE'S NOT ONLY AN OLD GEEZER, HE'S AN OLD GEEK, TOO!
HEY, I WAS JUST AHEAD OF MY TIME! NOW BRING ME BACK MY PULPS, GOLDURNIT!

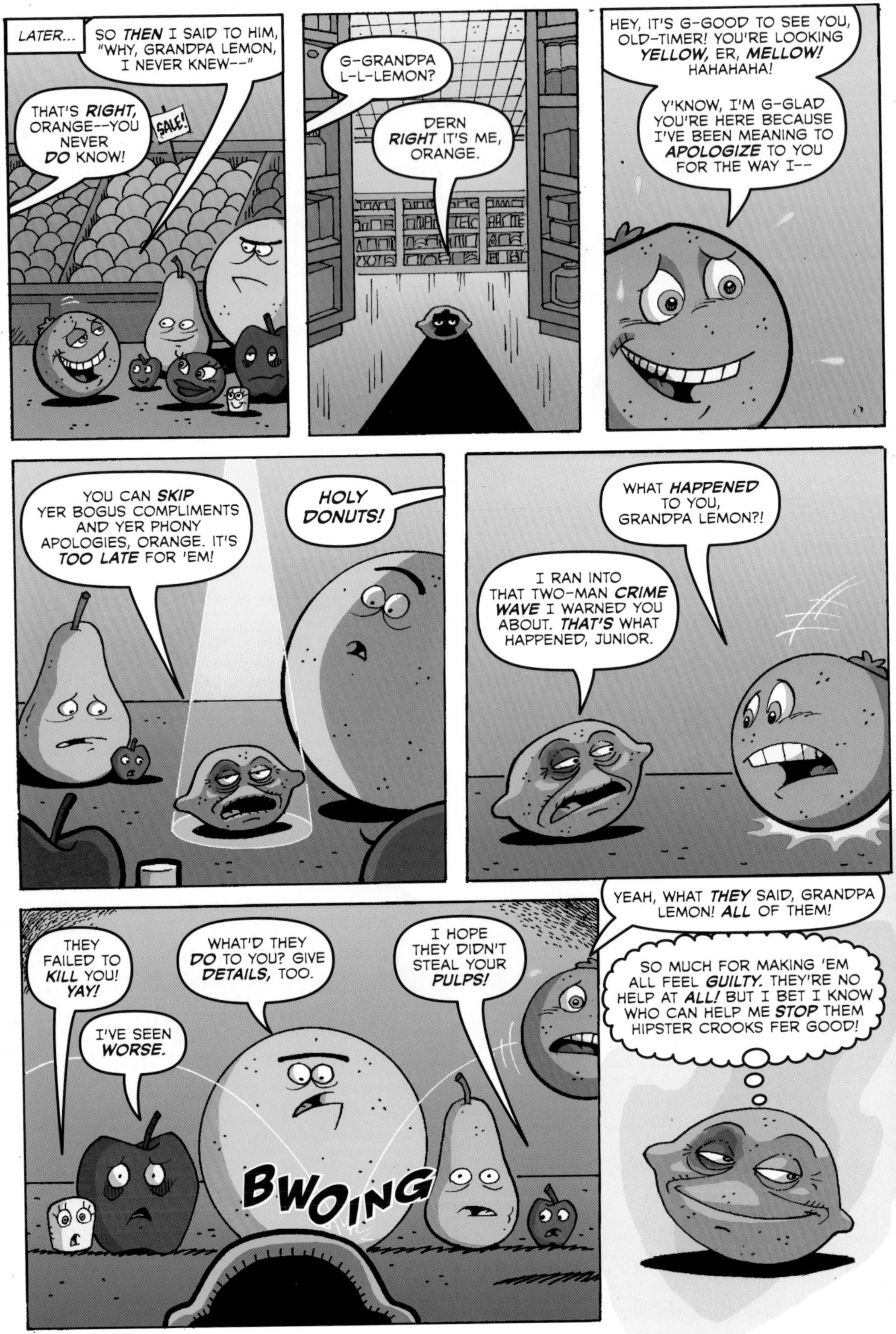
LATER...
SO THEN I SAID TO HIM, "WHY, GRANDPA LEMON, I NEVER KNEW--"
THAT'S RIGHT, ORANGE--YOU NEVER DO KNOW!
SALE!
G-GRANDPA L-L-LEMON?
DERN RIGHT IT'S ME, ORANGE.
HEY, IT'S G-GOOD TO SEE YOU, OLD-TIMER! YOU'RE LOOKING YELLOW, ER, MELLOW! HAHAHAHA!
Y'KNOW, I'M G-GLAD YOU'RE HERE BECAUSE I'VE BEEN MEANING TO APOLOGIZE TO YOU FOR THE WAY I--
YOU CAN SKIP YER BOGUS COMPLIMENTS AND YER PHONY APOLOGIES, ORANGE. IT'S TOO LATE FOR 'EM!
HOLY DONUTS!
WHAT HAPPENED TO YOU, GRANDPA LEMON?!
I RAN INTO THAT TWO-MAN CRIME WAVE I WARNED YOU ABOUT. THAT'S WHAT HAPPENED, JUNIOR.
THEY FAILED TO KILL YOU! YAY!
I'VE SEEN WORSE.
WHAT'D THEY DO TO YOU? GIVE DETAILS, TOO.
I HOPE THEY DIDN'T STEAL YOUR PULPS!
YEAH, WHAT THEY SAID, GRANDPA LEMON! ALL OF THEM!
BWOING
SO MUCH FOR MAKING 'EM ALL FEEL GUILTY. THEY'RE NO HELP AT ALL! BUT I BET I KNOW WHO CAN HELP ME STOP THEM HIPSTER CROOKS FER GOOD!

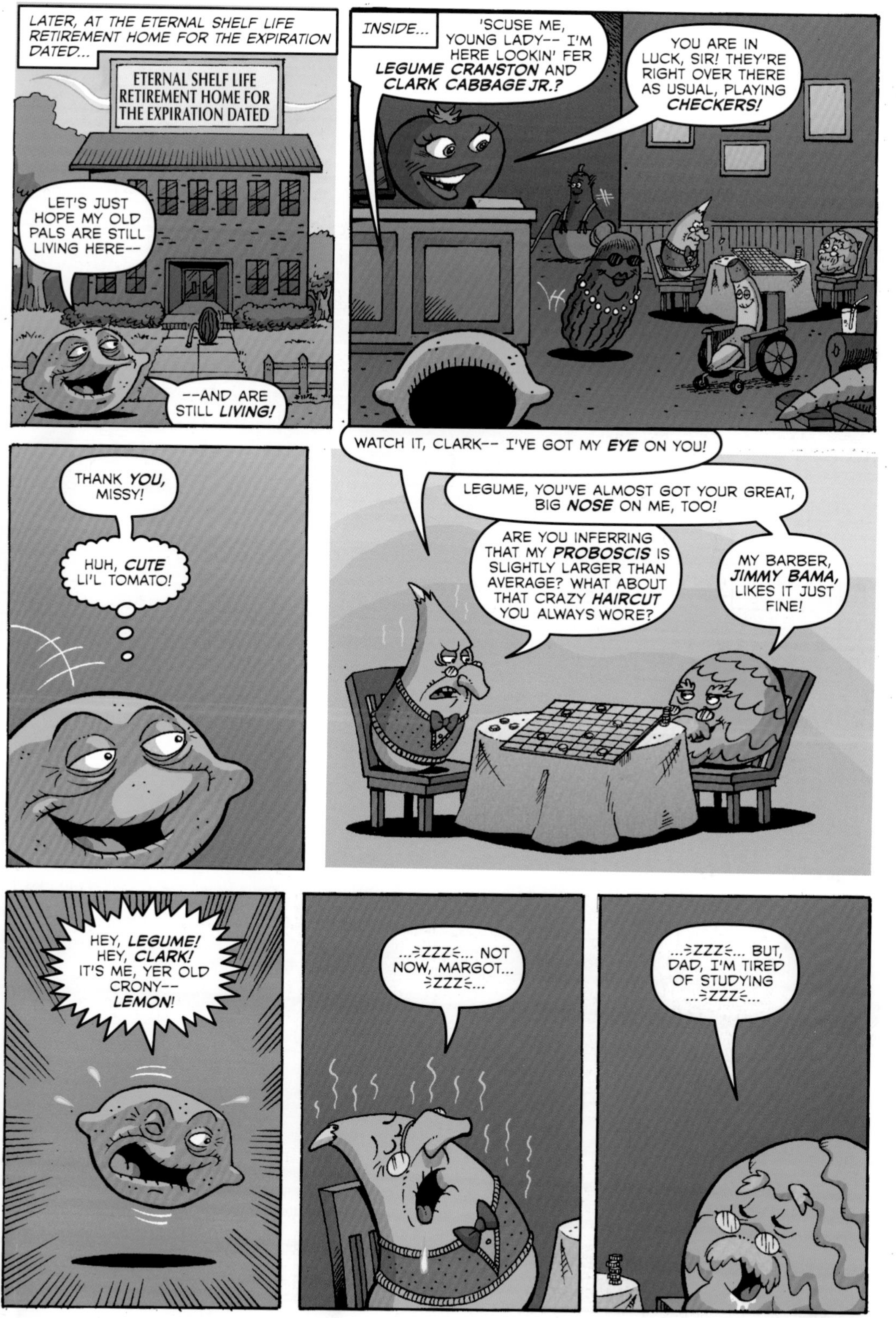
LATER, AT THE ETERNAL SHELF LIFE RETIREMENT HOME FOR THE EXPIRATION DATED...
ETERNAL SHELF LIFE RETIREMENT HOME FOR THE EXPIRATION DATED
LET'S JUST HOPE MY OLD PALS ARE STILL LIVING HERE--
--AND ARE STILL LIVING!
INSIDE...
'SCUSE ME, YOUNG LADY-- I'M HERE LOOKIN' FER LEGUME CRANSTON AND CLARK CABBAGE JR.?
YOU ARE IN LUCK, SIR! THEY'RE RIGHT OVER THERE AS USUAL, PLAYING CHECKERS!
THANK YOU, MISSY!
HUH, CUTE LI'L TOMATO!
WATCH IT, CLARK-- I'VE GOT MY EYE ON YOU!
LEGUME, YOU'VE ALMOST GOT YOUR GREAT, BIG NOSE ON ME, TOO!
ARE YOU INFERRING THAT MY PROBOSCIS IS SLIGHTLY LARGER THAN AVERAGE? WHAT ABOUT THAT CRAZY HAIRCUT YOU ALWAYS WORE?
MY BARBER, JIMMY BAMA, LIKES IT JUST FINE!
HEY, LEGUME! HEY, CLARK! IT'S ME, YER OLD CRONY-- LEMON!
...ZZZ... NOT NOW, MARGOT... ZZZ...
...ZZZ... BUT, DAD, I'M TIRED OF STUDYING ...ZZZ...

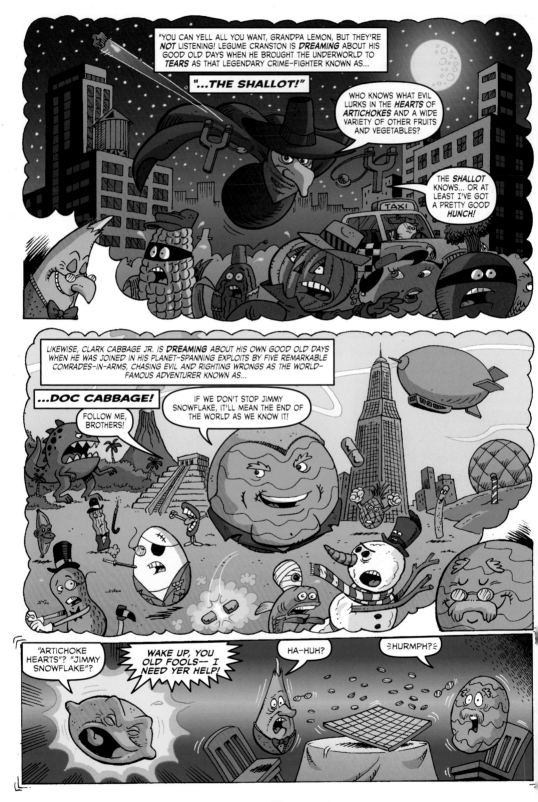

29

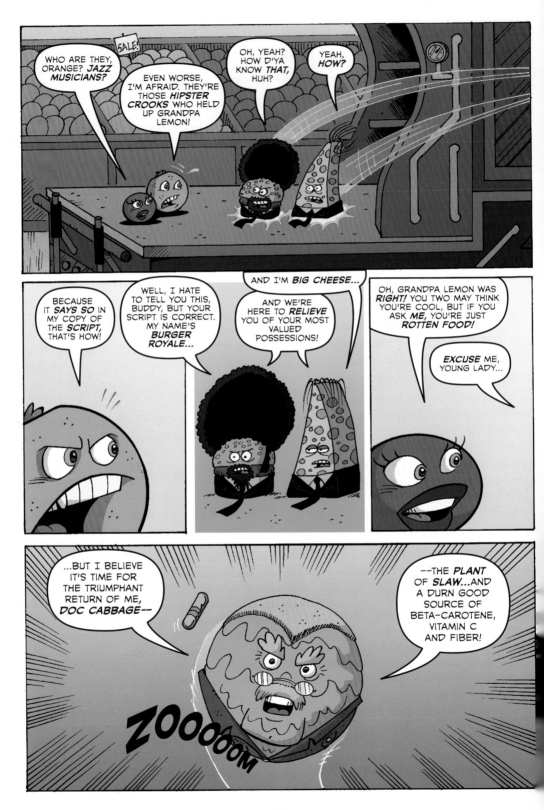

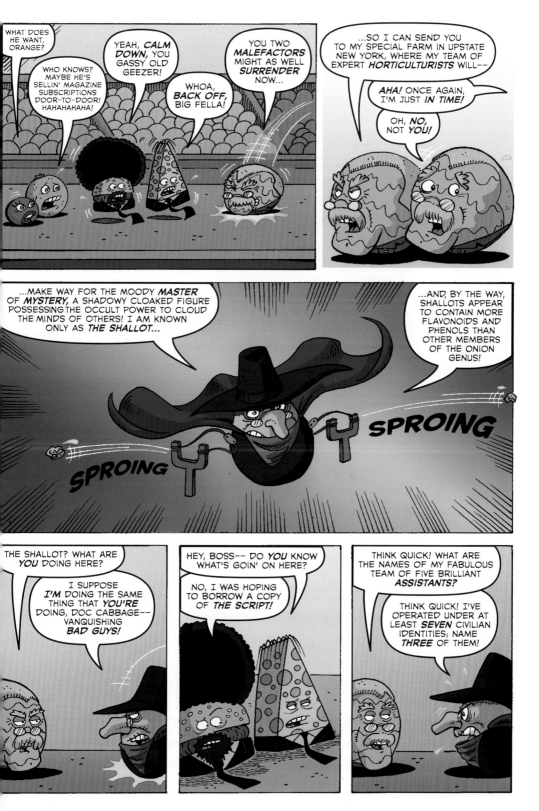

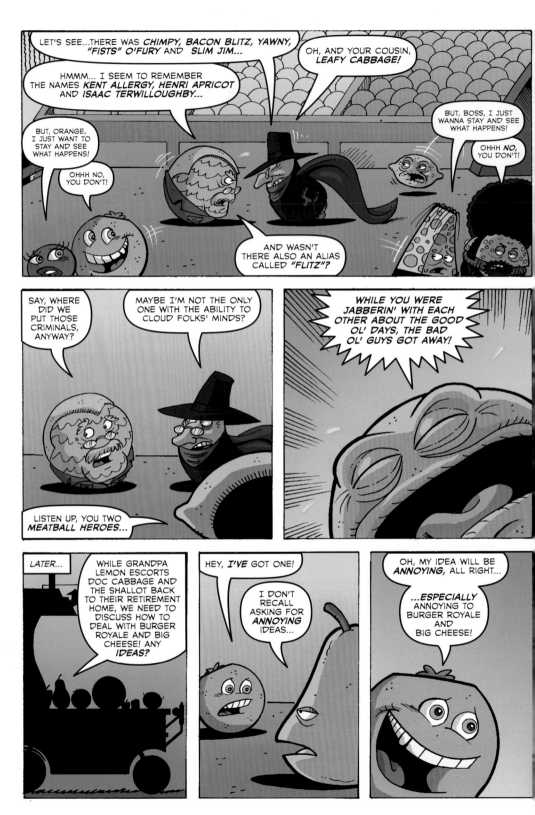

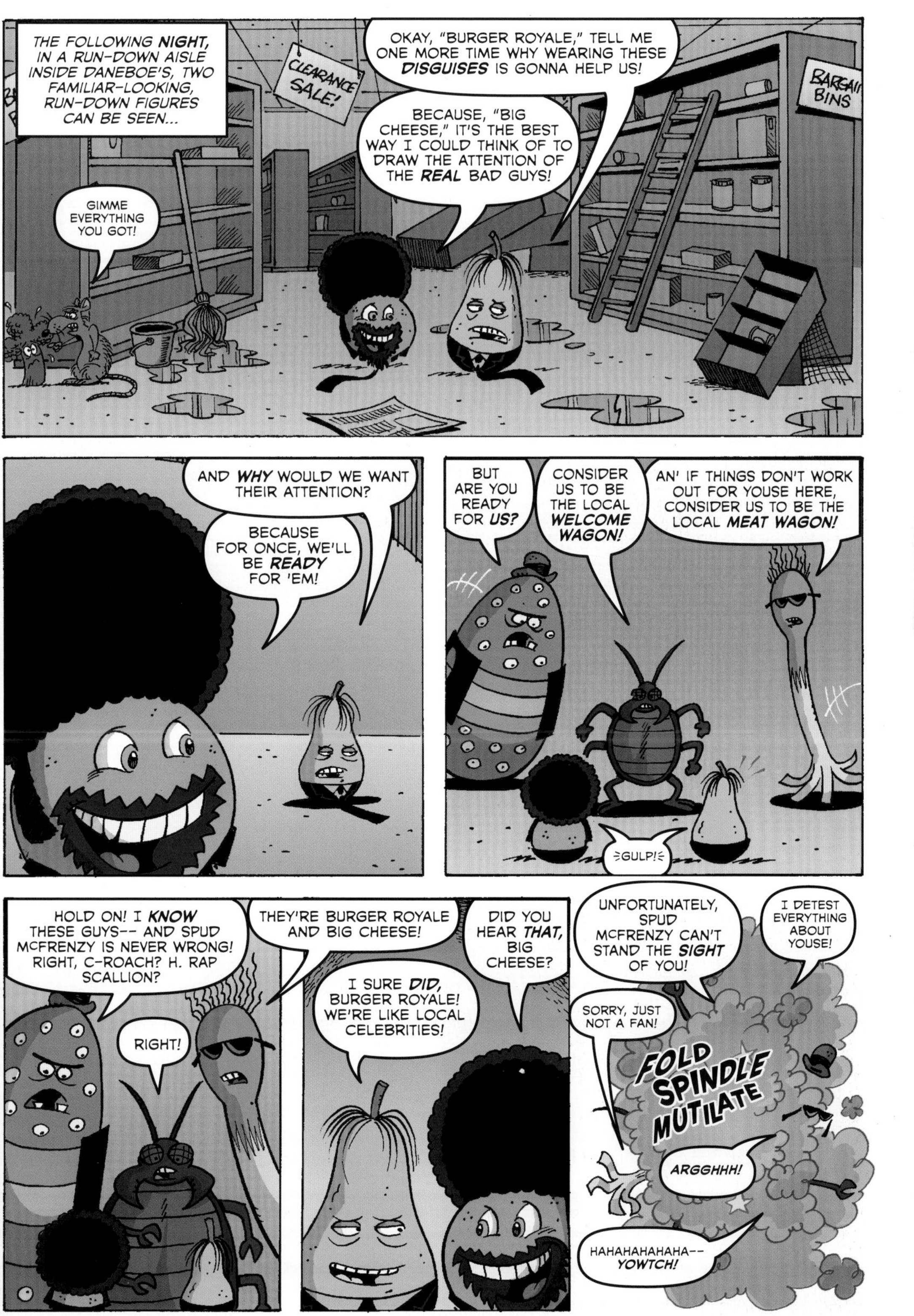
THE FOLLOWING NIGHT, IN A RUN-DOWN AISLE INSIDE DANEBOE'S, TWO FAMILIAR-LOOKING, RUN-DOWN FIGURES CAN BE SEEN...
CLEARANCE SALE!
OKAY, "BURGER ROYALE," TELL ME ONE MORE TIME WHY WEARING THESE DISGUISES IS GONNA HELP US!
BARGAIN BINS
BECAUSE, "BIG CHEESE," IT'S THE BEST WAY I COULD THINK OF TO DRAW THE ATTENTION OF THE REAL BAD GUYS!
GIMME EVERYTHING YOU GOT!
AND WHY WOULD WE WANT THEIR ATTENTION?
BECAUSE FOR ONCE, WE'LL BE READY FOR 'EM!
BUT ARE YOU READY FOR US?
CONSIDER US TO BE THE LOCAL WELCOME WAGON!
AN' IF THINGS DON'T WORK OUT FOR YOUSE HERE, CONSIDER US TO BE THE LOCAL MEAT WAGON!
GULP!
HOLD ON! I KNOW THESE GUYS-- AND SPUD McFRENZY IS NEVER WRONG! RIGHT, C-ROACH? H. RAP SCALLION?
RIGHT!
THEY'RE BURGER ROYALE AND BIG CHEESE!
DID YOU HEAR THAT, BIG CHEESE?
I SURE DID, BURGER ROYALE! WE'RE LIKE LOCAL CELEBRITIES!
UNFORTUNATELY, SPUD McFRENZY CAN'T STAND THE SIGHT OF YOU!
I DETEST EVERYTHING ABOUT YOUSE!
SORRY, JUST NOT A FAN!
FOLD SPINDLE MUTILATE
ARGGHHH!
HAHAHAHAHAHA-- YOWTCH!

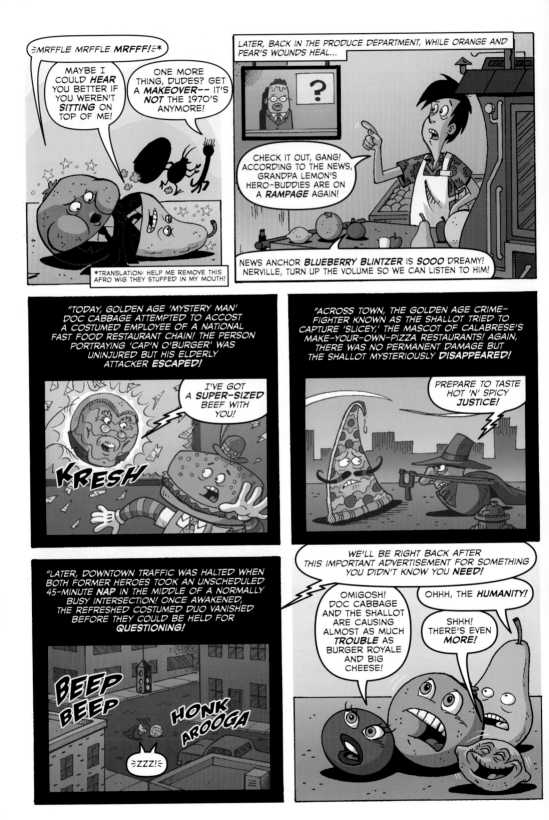

WE'RE GETTING NOWHERE **FAST!**

WAHHH!

"THIS IS BLUEBERRY BLINTZER, BACK WITH MORE ON THE RECENT **RAMPAGE** BY A PAIR OF SEPTUAGENARIAN HEROES! HERE'S FOOTAGE OF DOC CABBAGE AND THE SHALLOT COMMANDEERING A 'VEHICLE' ON ONE OF THOSE COIN-OPERATED KIDDIE RIDES! FORTUNATELY, BEFORE LONG, THEY RAN OUT OF **QUARTERS!**"

"THEN, IN AN EFFORT TO PROVE THAT HE POSSESSES THE MYSTERIOUS 'POWER TO CLOUD MEN'S MINDS,' THE SHALLOT ACCIDENTALLY PUT HIMSELF INTO A **HYPNOTIC DAZE!** AT THE SAME TIME, DOC CABBAGE FELL INTO A SIMILAR CONDITION WHEN HE MISTAKENLY ACTIVATED ONE OF HIS **ANAESTHETIC GAS BOMBS!** THEIR NUMBED BRAINS WERE RELEASED FROM THEIR DEEP TRANCES ONLY WHEN THE GERIATRIC 'MYSTERY MEN' OVERHEARD THE MUSIC FROM A PASSING ICE CREAM TRUCK!"

ZAP!

"AND MOST RECENTLY, DOC CABBAGE AND THE SHALLOT SHOWED UP HERE AT OUR NEWS STUDIO, WHERE THEY'VE BEEN FLAGRANTLY DISRUPTING THIS BROADCAST, CLAIMING THAT WE'RE 'LEAKING INFORMATION TO THE ENEMY'! IF ANYONE'S OUT THERE WATCHING ME, THIS IS BLUEBERRY BLINTZER SAYING, **'HELP! GET THOSE ELDERLY MANIACS OUT OF HERE!'** THANK YOU AND GOODNIGHT."

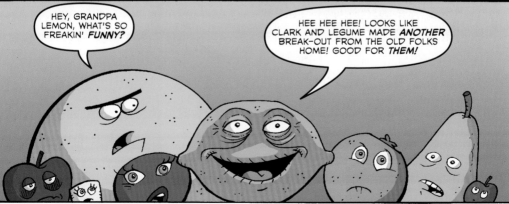

HEY, GRANDPA LEMON, WHAT'S SO FREAKIN' **FUNNY?**

HEE HEE HEE! LOOKS LIKE CLARK AND LEGUME MADE **ANOTHER** BREAK-OUT FROM THE OLD FOLKS HOME! GOOD FOR **THEM!**

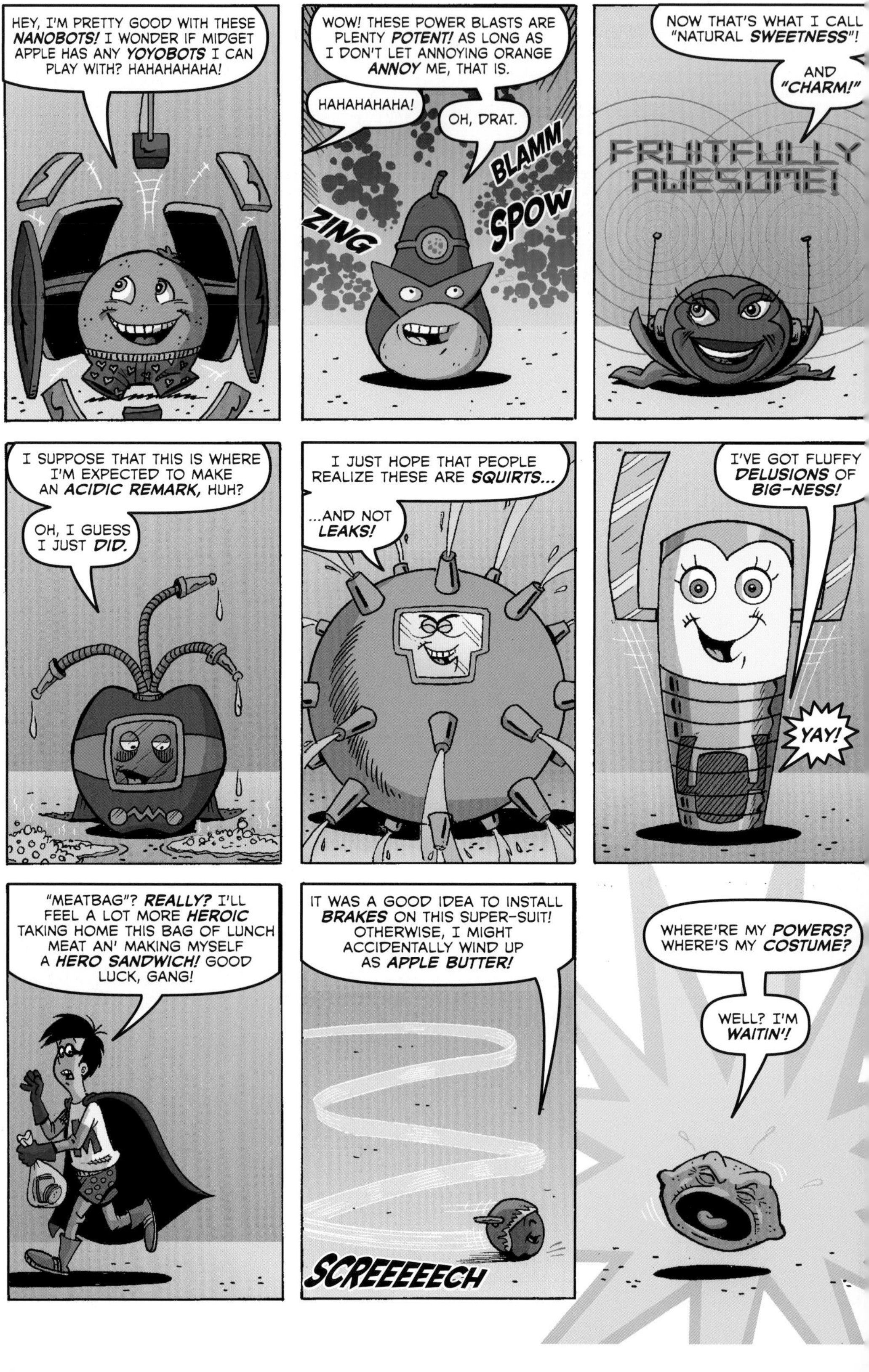
HEY, I'M PRETTY GOOD WITH THESE NANOBOTS! I WONDER IF MIDGET APPLE HAS ANY YOYOBOTS I CAN PLAY WITH? HAHAHAHAHA!
WOW! THESE POWER BLASTS ARE PLENTY POTENT! AS LONG AS I DON'T LET ANNOYING ORANGE ANNOY ME, THAT IS.
HAHAHAHAHA!
OH, DRAT.
BLAMM
ZING
SPOW
NOW THAT'S WHAT I CALL "NATURAL SWEETNESS"!
AND "CHARM!"
FRUITFULLY AWESOME!
I SUPPOSE THAT THIS IS WHERE I'M EXPECTED TO MAKE AN ACIDIC REMARK, HUH?
OH, I GUESS I JUST DID.
I JUST HOPE THAT PEOPLE REALIZE THESE ARE SQUIRTS...
...AND NOT LEAKS!
I'VE GOT FLUFFY DELUSIONS OF BIG-NESS!
YAY!
"MEATBAG"? REALLY? I'LL FEEL A LOT MORE HEROIC TAKING HOME THIS BAG OF LUNCH MEAT AN' MAKING MYSELF A HERO SANDWICH! GOOD LUCK, GANG!
IT WAS A GOOD IDEA TO INSTALL BRAKES ON THIS SUPER-SUIT! OTHERWISE, I MIGHT ACCIDENTALLY WIND UP AS APPLE BUTTER!
SCREEEEEECH
WHERE'RE MY POWERS? WHERE'S MY COSTUME?
WELL? I'M WAITIN'!

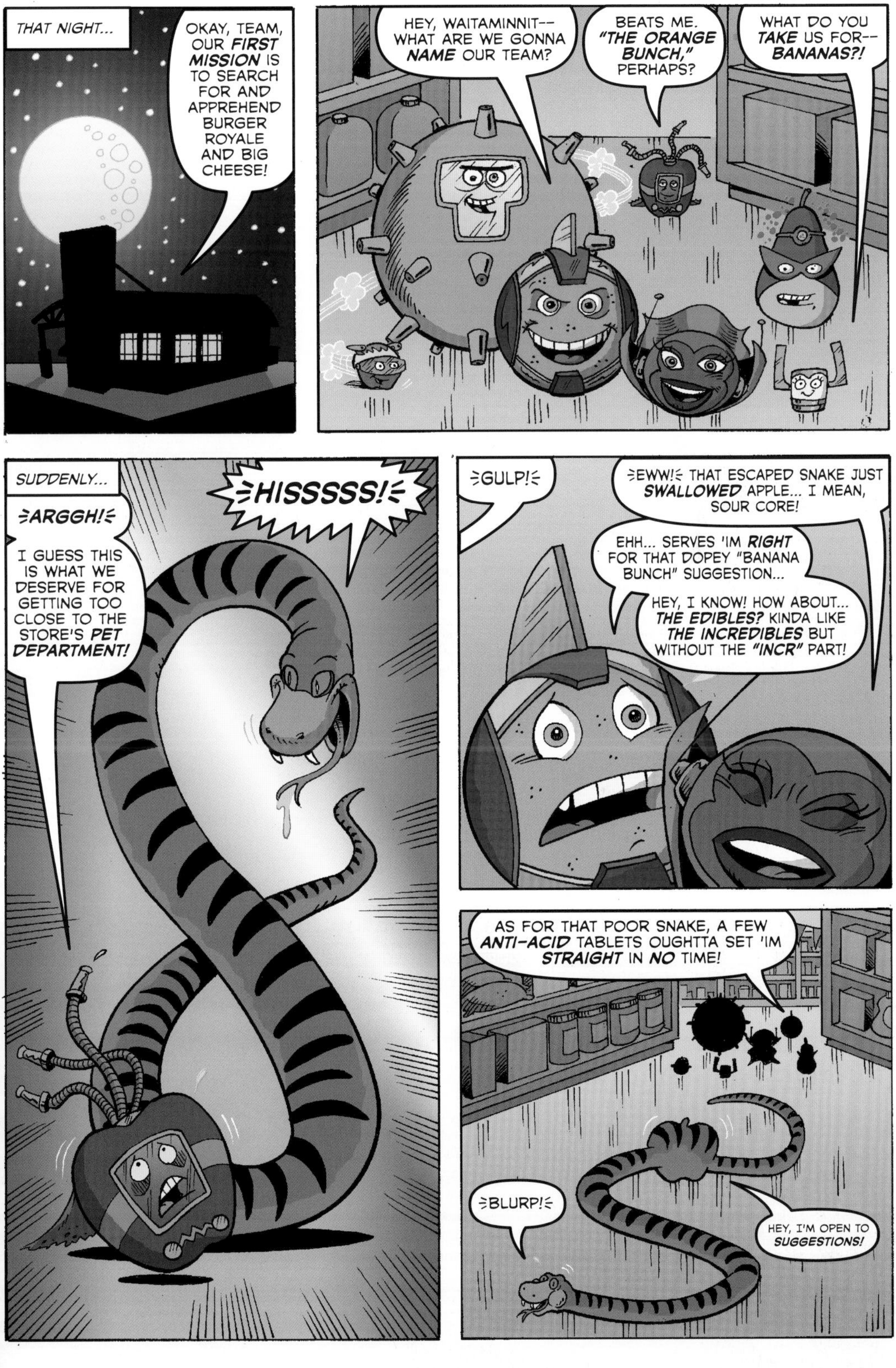
THAT NIGHT...
OKAY, TEAM, OUR FIRST MISSION IS TO SEARCH FOR AND APPREHEND BURGER ROYALE AND BIG CHEESE!
HEY, WAITAMINNIT-- WHAT ARE WE GONNA NAME OUR TEAM?
BEATS ME. "THE ORANGE BUNCH," PERHAPS?
WHAT DO YOU TAKE US FOR-- BANANAS?!
SUDDENLY...
HISSSSS!
ARGGH!
I GUESS THIS IS WHAT WE DESERVE FOR GETTING TOO CLOSE TO THE STORE'S PET DEPARTMENT!
GULP!
EWW! THAT ESCAPED SNAKE JUST SWALLOWED APPLE... I MEAN, SOUR CORE!
EHH... SERVES 'IM RIGHT FOR THAT DOPEY "BANANA BUNCH" SUGGESTION...
HEY, I KNOW! HOW ABOUT... THE EDIBLES? KINDA LIKE THE INCREDIBLES BUT WITHOUT THE "INCR" PART!
AS FOR THAT POOR SNAKE, A FEW ANTI-ACID TABLETS OUGHTTA SET 'IM STRAIGHT IN NO TIME!
BLURP!
HEY, I'M OPEN TO SUGGESTIONS!

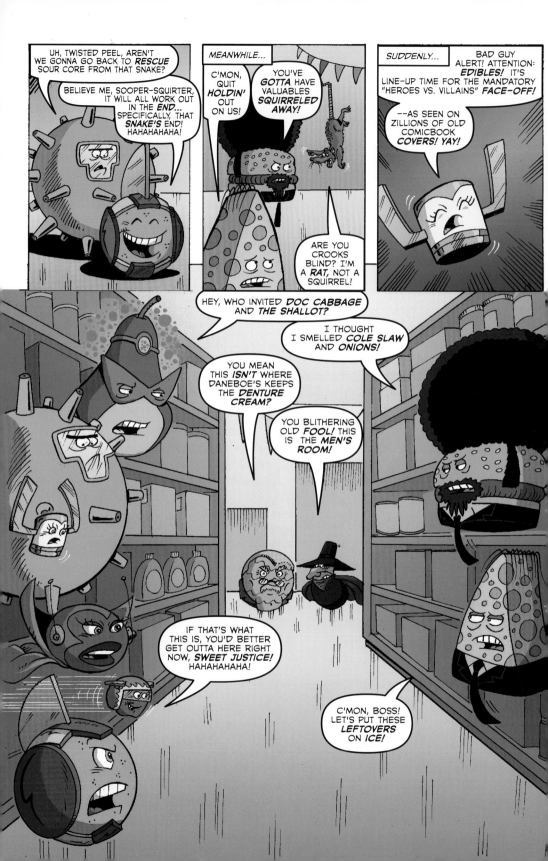

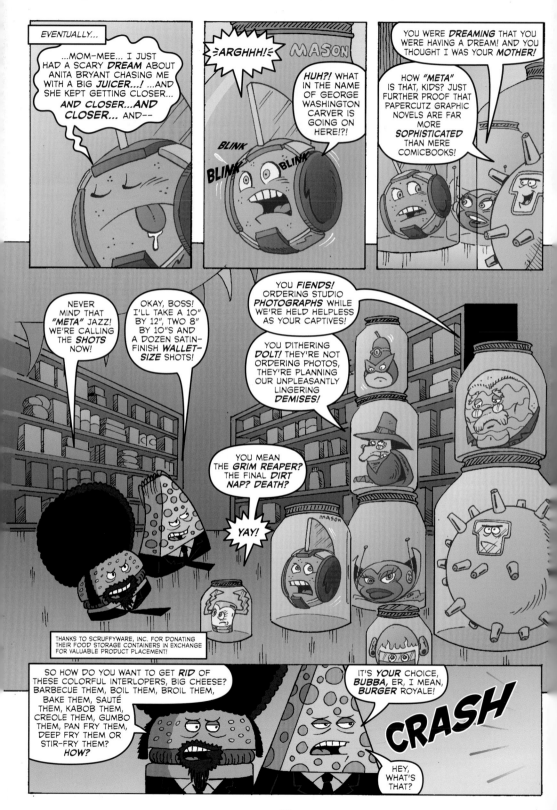

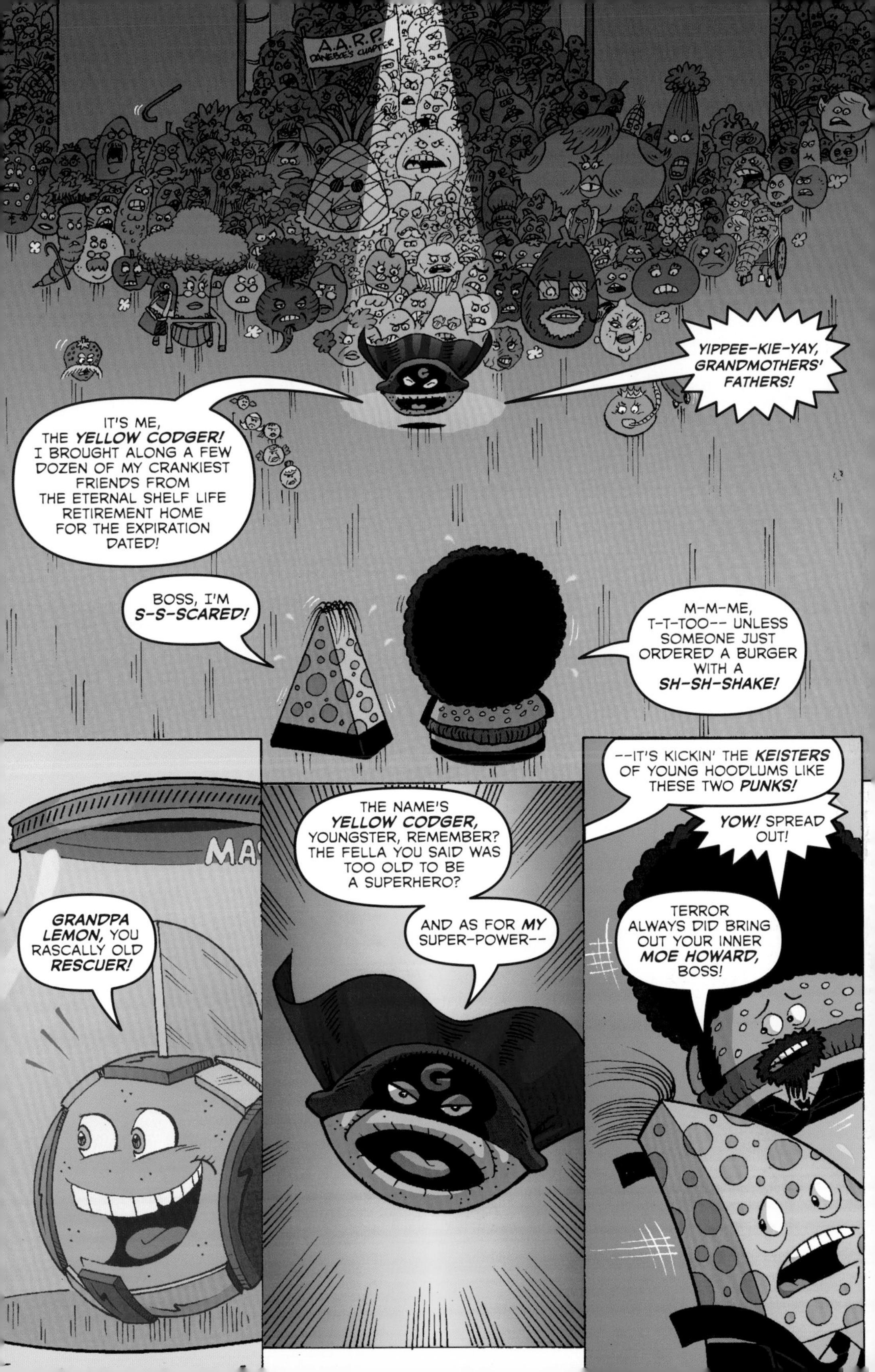
A.A.R.P. DANEBOE'S CHAPTER
YIPPEE-KIE-YAY, GRANDMOTHERS' FATHERS!
IT'S ME, THE YELLOW CODGER! I BROUGHT ALONG A FEW DOZEN OF MY CRANKIEST FRIENDS FROM THE ETERNAL SHELF LIFE RETIREMENT HOME FOR THE EXPIRATION DATED!
BOSS, I'M S-S-SCARED!
M-M-ME, T-T-TOO-- UNLESS SOMEONE JUST ORDERED A BURGER WITH A SH-SH-SHAKE!
GRANDPA LEMON, YOU RASCALLY OLD RESCUER!
THE NAME'S YELLOW CODGER, YOUNGSTER, REMEMBER? THE FELLA YOU SAID WAS TOO OLD TO BE A SUPERHERO?
AND AS FOR MY SUPER-POWER--
--IT'S KICKIN' THE KEISTERS OF YOUNG HOODLUMS LIKE THESE TWO PUNKS!
YOW! SPREAD OUT!
TERROR ALWAYS DID BRING OUT YOUR INNER MOE HOWARD, BOSS!

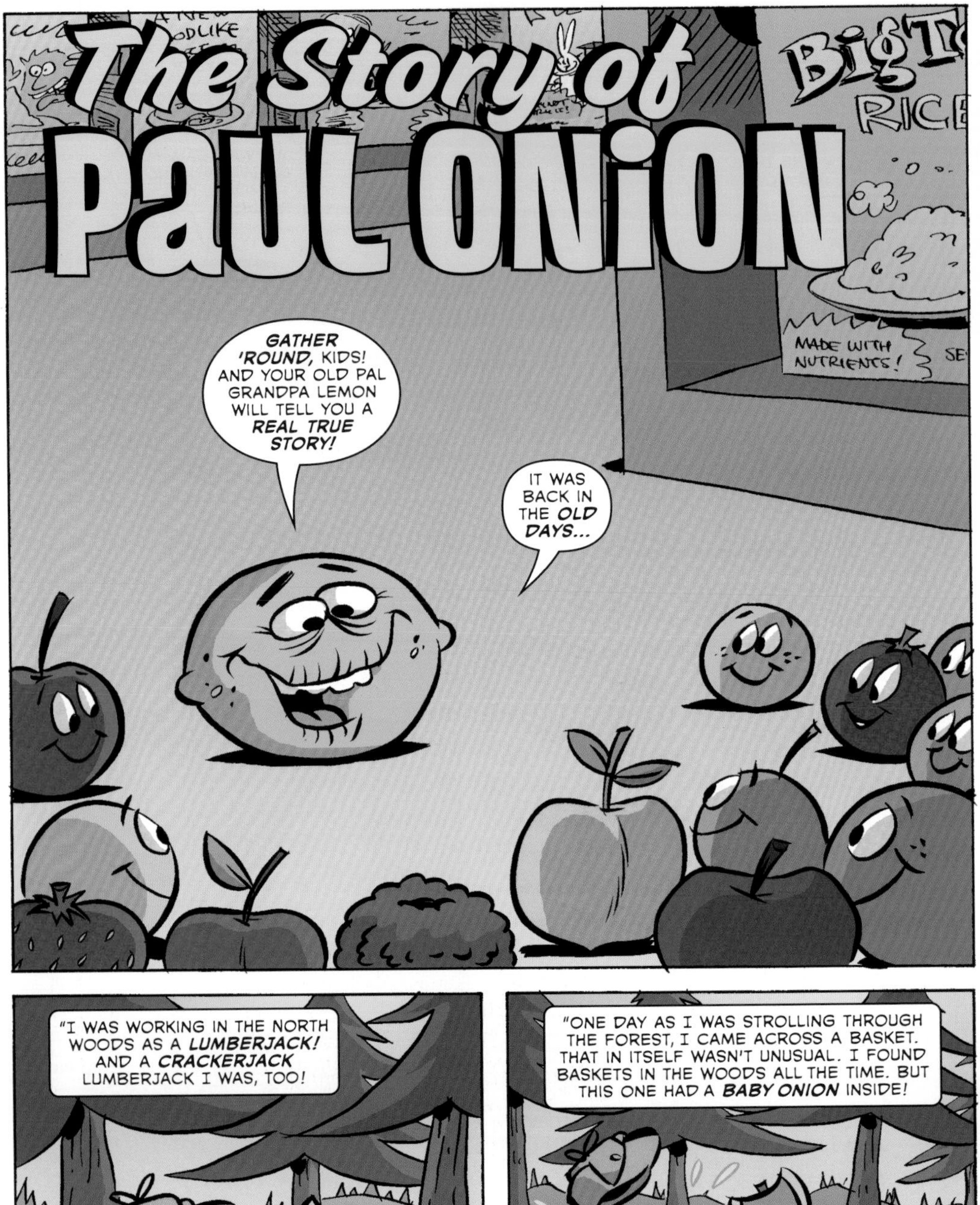

The Story of PAUL ONION
RICE
MADE WITH NUTRIENTS!
GATHER 'ROUND, KIDS! AND YOUR OLD PAL GRANDPA LEMON WILL TELL YOU A REAL TRUE STORY!
IT WAS BACK IN THE OLD DAYS...
"I WAS WORKING IN THE NORTH WOODS AS A LUMBERJACK! AND A CRACKERJACK LUMBERJACK I WAS, TOO!
"ONE DAY AS I WAS STROLLING THROUGH THE FOREST, I CAME ACROSS A BASKET. THAT IN ITSELF WASN'T UNUSUAL. I FOUND BASKETS IN THE WOODS ALL THE TIME. BUT THIS ONE HAD A BABY ONION INSIDE!

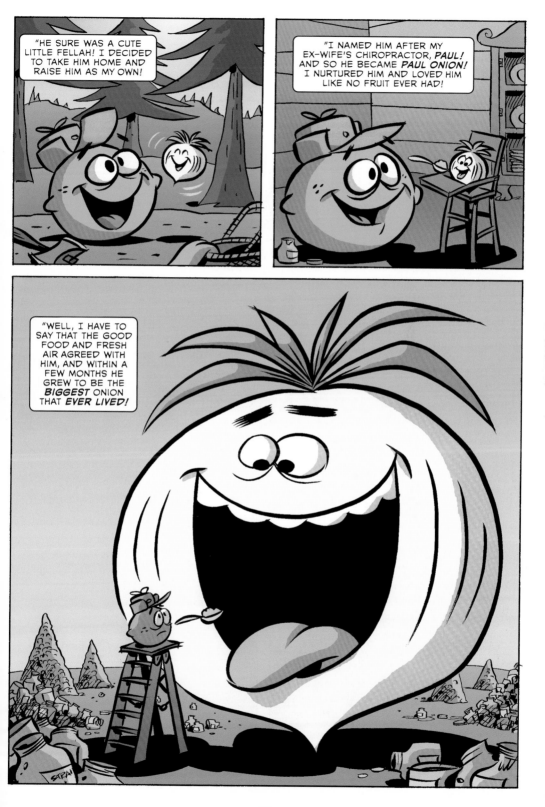

"HE SURE WAS A CUTE LITTLE FELLAH! I DECIDED TO TAKE HIM HOME AND RAISE HIM AS MY OWN!"

"I NAMED HIM AFTER MY EX-WIFE'S CHIROPRACTOR, PAUL! AND SO HE BECAME PAUL ONION! I NURTURED HIM AND LOVED HIM LIKE NO FRUIT EVER HAD!"

"WELL, I HAVE TO SAY THAT THE GOOD FOOD AND FRESH AIR AGREED WITH HIM, AND WITHIN A FEW MONTHS HE GREW TO BE THE BIGGEST ONION THAT EVER LIVED!"

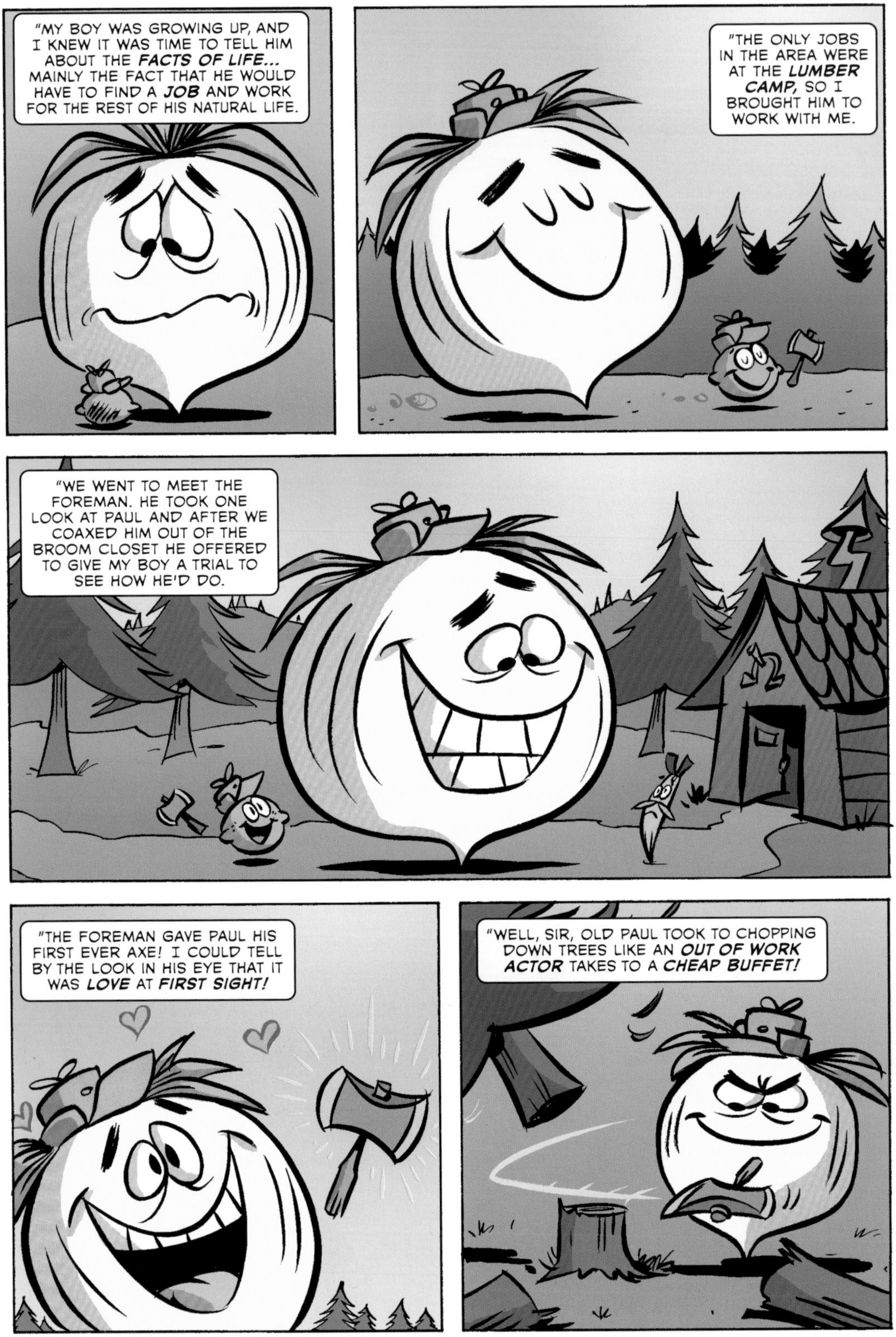
"MY BOY WAS GROWING UP, AND I KNEW IT WAS TIME TO TELL HIM ABOUT THE **FACTS OF LIFE...** MAINLY THE FACT THAT HE WOULD HAVE TO FIND A **JOB** AND WORK FOR THE REST OF HIS NATURAL LIFE.
"THE ONLY JOBS IN THE AREA WERE AT THE **LUMBER CAMP,** SO I BROUGHT HIM TO WORK WITH ME.
"WE WENT TO MEET THE FOREMAN. HE TOOK ONE LOOK AT PAUL AND AFTER WE COAXED HIM OUT OF THE BROOM CLOSET HE OFFERED TO GIVE MY BOY A TRIAL TO SEE HOW HE'D DO.
"THE FOREMAN GAVE PAUL HIS FIRST EVER AXE! I COULD TELL BY THE LOOK IN HIS EYE THAT IT WAS **LOVE** AT **FIRST SIGHT!**
"WELL, SIR, OLD PAUL TOOK TO CHOPPING DOWN TREES LIKE AN **OUT OF WORK ACTOR** TAKES TO A **CHEAP BUFFET!**

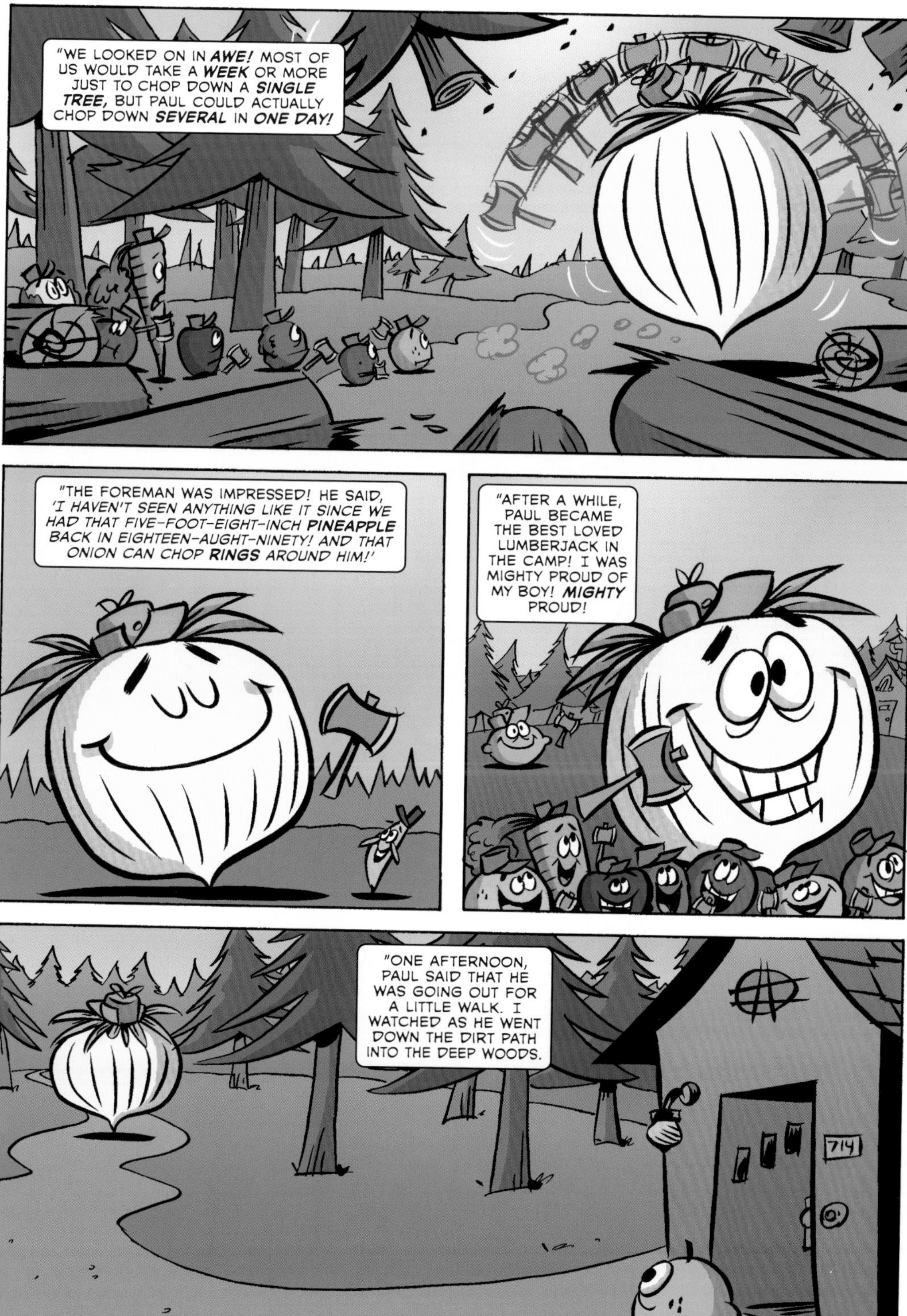
"WE LOOKED ON IN AWE! MOST OF US WOULD TAKE A WEEK OR MORE JUST TO CHOP DOWN A SINGLE TREE, BUT PAUL COULD ACTUALLY CHOP DOWN SEVERAL IN ONE DAY!
"THE FOREMAN WAS IMPRESSED! HE SAID, 'I HAVEN'T SEEN ANYTHING LIKE IT SINCE WE HAD THAT FIVE-FOOT-EIGHT-INCH PINEAPPLE BACK IN EIGHTEEN-AUGHT-NINETY! AND THAT ONION CAN CHOP RINGS AROUND HIM!'
"AFTER A WHILE, PAUL BECAME THE BEST LOVED LUMBERJACK IN THE CAMP! I WAS MIGHTY PROUD OF MY BOY! MIGHTY PROUD!
"ONE AFTERNOON, PAUL SAID THAT HE WAS GOING OUT FOR A LITTLE WALK. I WATCHED AS HE WENT DOWN THE DIRT PATH INTO THE DEEP WOODS.
714

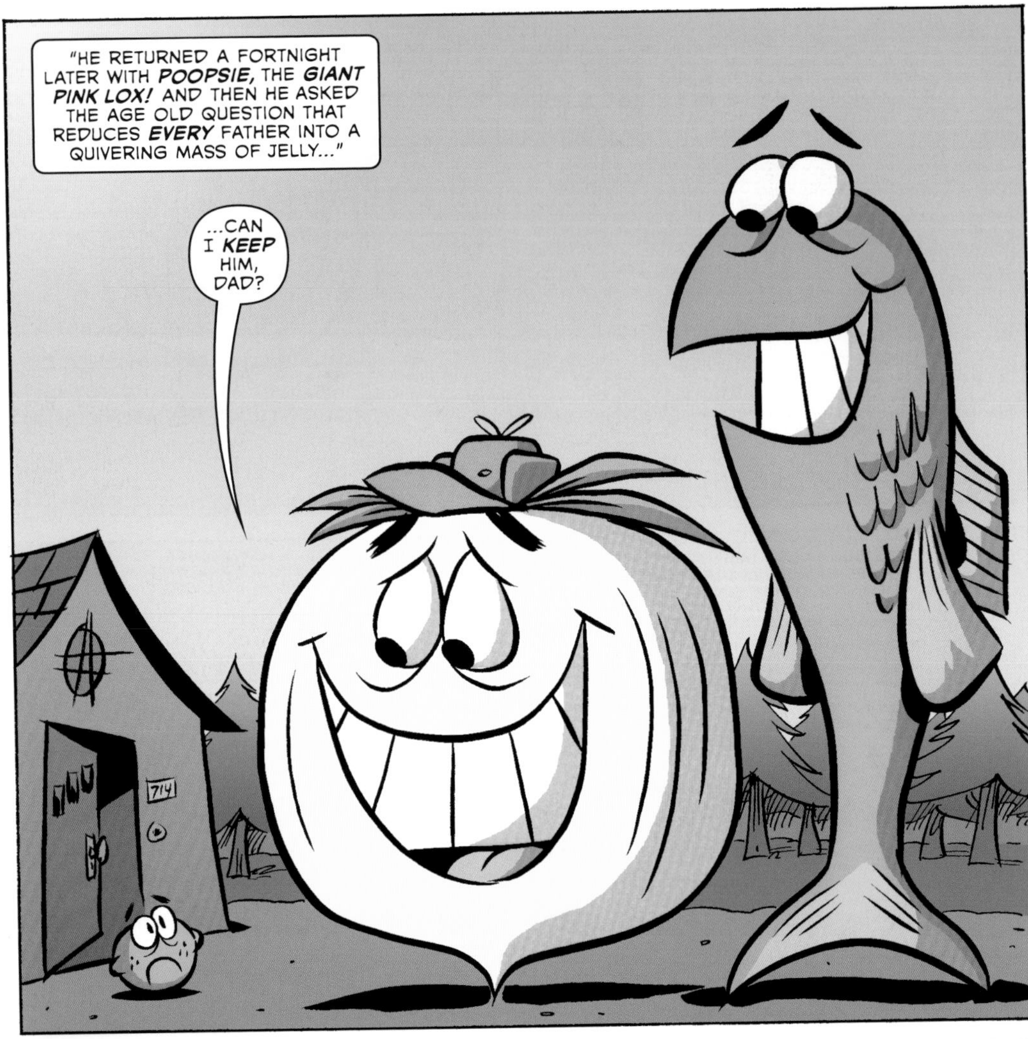
"HE RETURNED A FORTNIGHT LATER WITH POOPSIE, THE GIANT PINK LOX! AND THEN HE ASKED THE AGE OLD QUESTION THAT REDUCES EVERY FATHER INTO A QUIVERING MASS OF JELLY..."
...CAN I KEEP HIM, DAD?
714

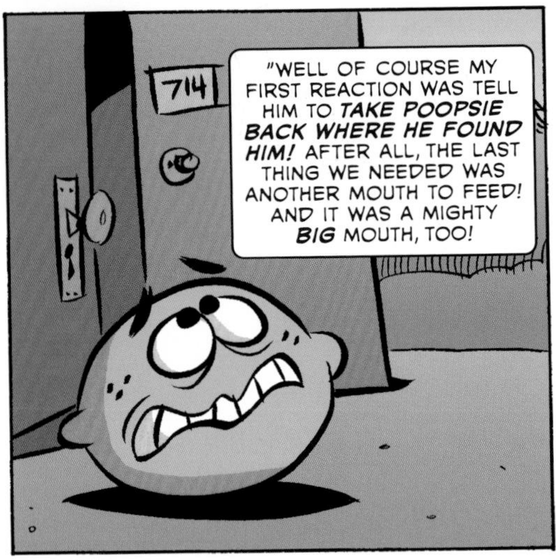
714
"WELL OF COURSE MY FIRST REACTION WAS TELL HIM TO TAKE POOPSIE BACK WHERE HE FOUND HIM! AFTER ALL, THE LAST THING WE NEEDED WAS ANOTHER MOUTH TO FEED! AND IT WAS A MIGHTY BIG MOUTH, TOO!

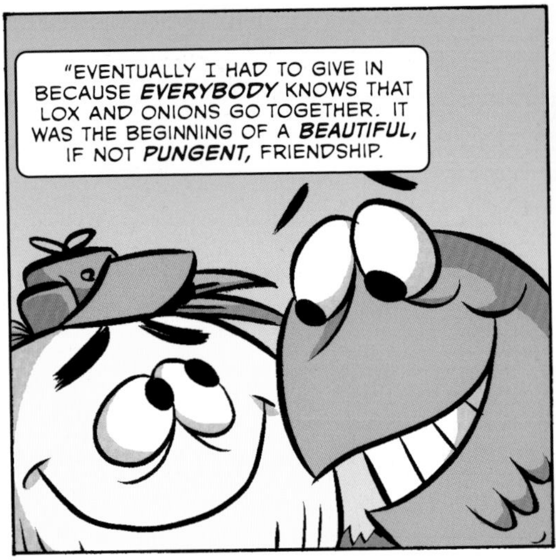
"EVENTUALLY I HAD TO GIVE IN BECAUSE EVERYBODY KNOWS THAT LOX AND ONIONS GO TOGETHER. IT WAS THE BEGINNING OF A BEAUTIFUL, IF NOT PUNGENT, FRIENDSHIP.

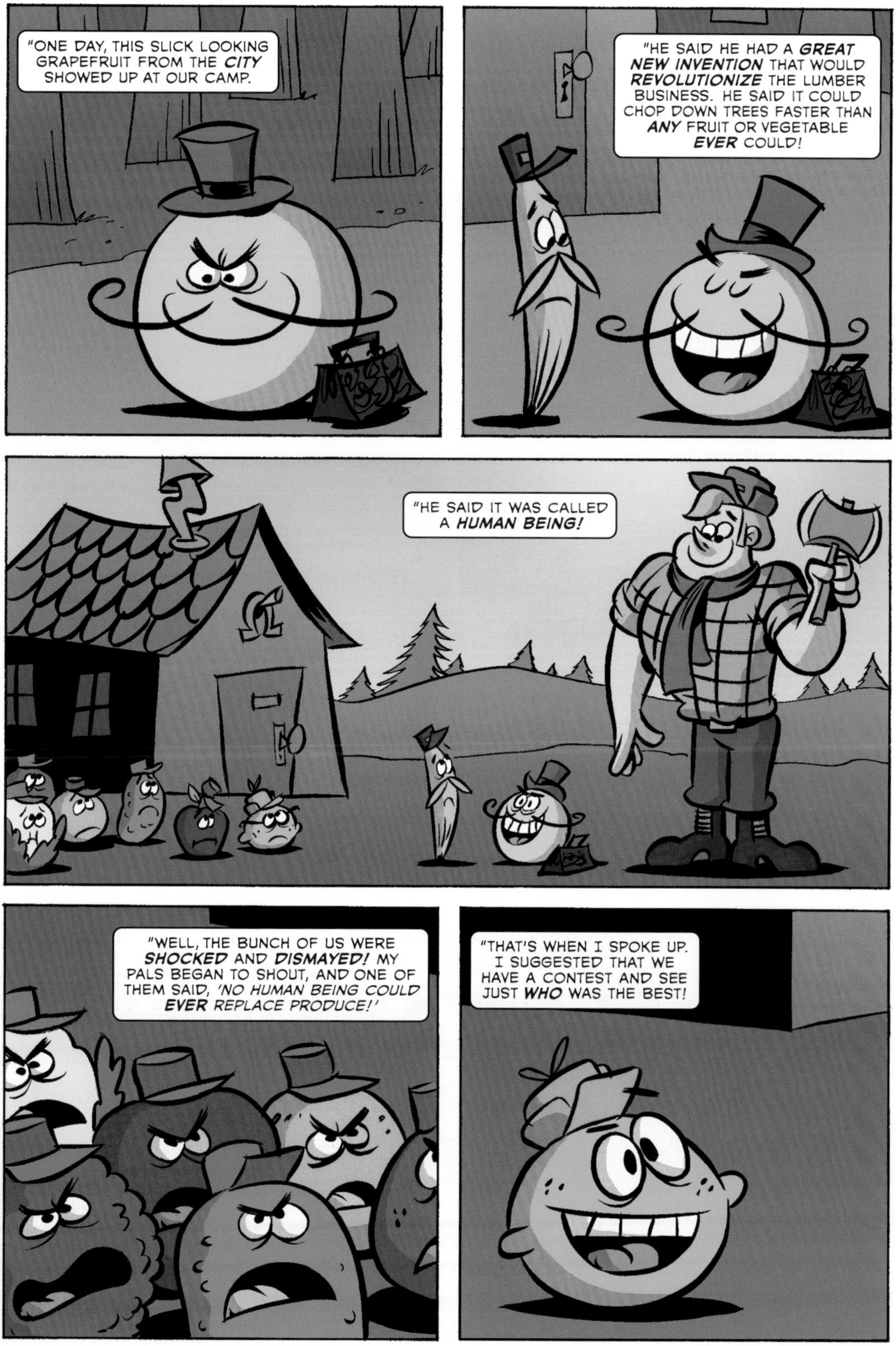
"ONE DAY, THIS SLICK LOOKING GRAPEFRUIT FROM THE *CITY* SHOWED UP AT OUR CAMP.
"HE SAID HE HAD A ***GREAT NEW INVENTION*** THAT WOULD ***REVOLUTIONIZE*** THE LUMBER BUSINESS. HE SAID IT COULD CHOP DOWN TREES FASTER THAN ***ANY*** FRUIT OR VEGETABLE ***EVER*** COULD!
"HE SAID IT WAS CALLED A ***HUMAN BEING!***
"WELL, THE BUNCH OF US WERE ***SHOCKED*** AND ***DISMAYED!*** MY PALS BEGAN TO SHOUT, AND ONE OF THEM SAID, *'NO HUMAN BEING COULD* ***EVER*** *REPLACE PRODUCE!'*
"THAT'S WHEN I SPOKE UP. I SUGGESTED THAT WE HAVE A CONTEST AND SEE JUST ***WHO*** WAS THE BEST!

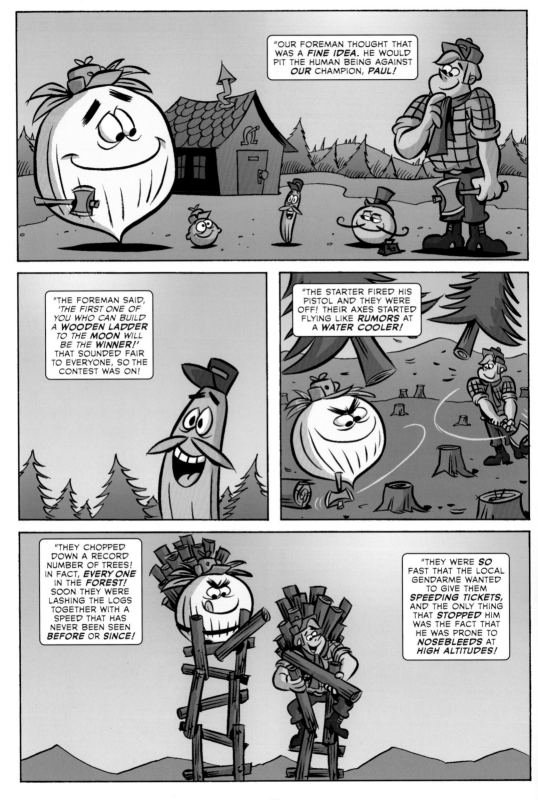

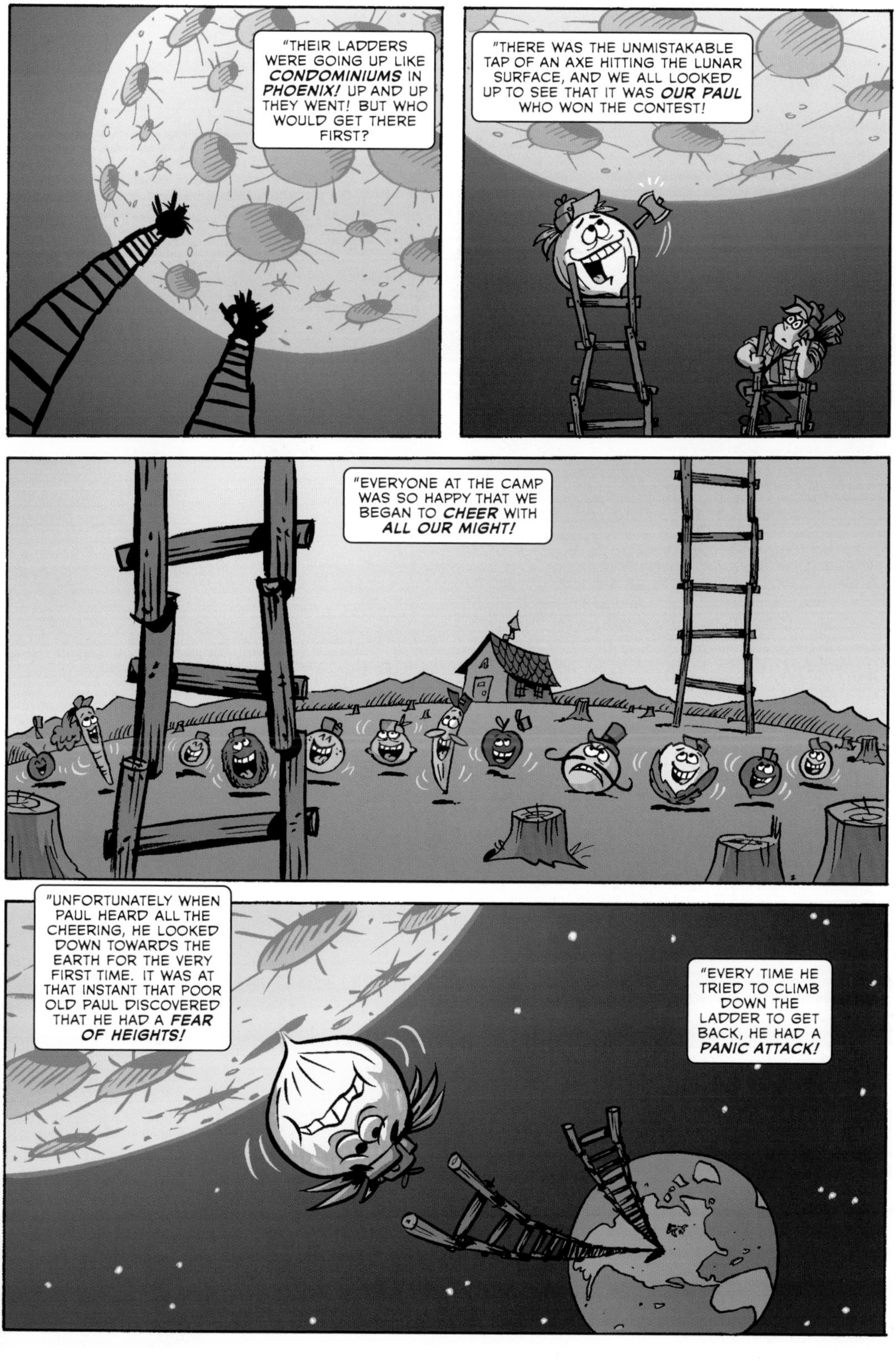
"THEIR LADDERS WERE GOING UP LIKE CONDOMINIUMS IN PHOENIX! UP AND UP THEY WENT! BUT WHO WOULD GET THERE FIRST?
"THERE WAS THE UNMISTAKABLE TAP OF AN AXE HITTING THE LUNAR SURFACE, AND WE ALL LOOKED UP TO SEE THAT IT WAS OUR PAUL WHO WON THE CONTEST!
"EVERYONE AT THE CAMP WAS SO HAPPY THAT WE BEGAN TO CHEER WITH ALL OUR MIGHT!
"UNFORTUNATELY WHEN PAUL HEARD ALL THE CHEERING, HE LOOKED DOWN TOWARDS THE EARTH FOR THE VERY FIRST TIME. IT WAS AT THAT INSTANT THAT POOR OLD PAUL DISCOVERED THAT HE HAD A FEAR OF HEIGHTS!
"EVERY TIME HE TRIED TO CLIMB DOWN THE LADDER TO GET BACK, HE HAD A PANIC ATTACK!

DANE BOEDIGHEIMER

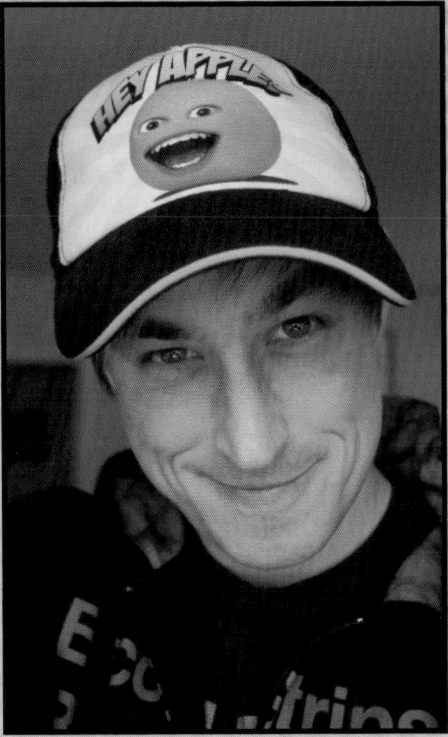

Dane (or Daneboe as he's known online) is a filmmaker and goofball extraordinaire. Dane spent most of his life in the glamorous Midwest, Harwood, North Dakota, to be exact. With nothing better to do, (it was North Dakota) at around the age of twelve, Dane began making short movies and videos with his parents' camcorder. Since then he has made hundreds, if not thousands of short web videos… many of which are only funny to him. But Dane has remained determined to make "the perfect short comedy film;" one that will end all social problems and bring laughter to all the children of the world.

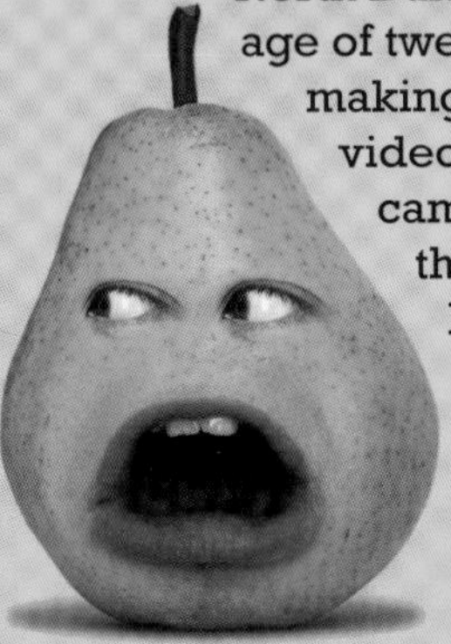

Currently, Dane is most widely known for creating The Annoying Orange, one of the most successful web series ever. The Annoying Orange has over 2 million subscribers and over 1 billion video views on YouTube as well as over 11 million facebook fans. On top of that, The Annoying Orange has a top rated show on Cartoon Network! As a result, fans have clamored for all sorts of cool Annoying Orange toys, t-shirts, games, etc. And despite all the wonderful stuff that has already appeared, fans still want more, and we suspect they'll be getting it.

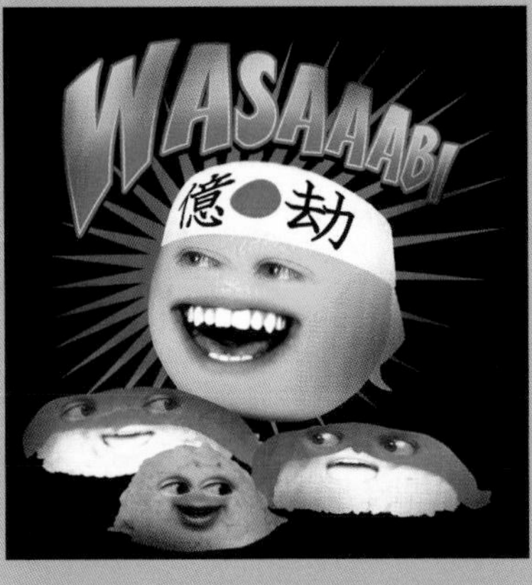
WASAAABI
億 劫

Not to be completely undone, Dane's other videos have been viewed over 650 million times and have been featured on TV, as well as some of the most popular entertainment, news, and video sharing sites on the Internet.

In Dane's downtime he enjoys… oh, who are we kidding? Dane doesn't have any downtime. He wouldn't know what to do with himself if he did.

SPENCER GROVE

Spencer Grove has written plays, prose, television scripts and more online videos than any sane person should attempt. Also, he bakes a mean apple pie.

He began his career in independent productions, working on everything from infomercials to award shows, eventually moving to MTV where he served as an Associate Producer on Pimp My Ride. Since 2009, he has served as the head writer of the Annoying Orange web series, creating and co-creating the supporting cast and developing the ever-expanding online world of the Orange.

TOM SHEPPARD

Tom Sheppard is a multiple Emmy-award winning talking animal wordsmith. He's written for all manner of beasts, from genetically altered lab mice, to crazy barnyard animals, butt-obsessed monkeys and even the occasional human, such as the Green Lantern. Since diving into the world of Annoying Orange, it has been his pleasure to expand his repertoire to talking fruit. He is currently writing, producing and directing the live action/animated High Fructose Adventures of Annoying Orange for Cartoon Network.

SCOTT SHAW!

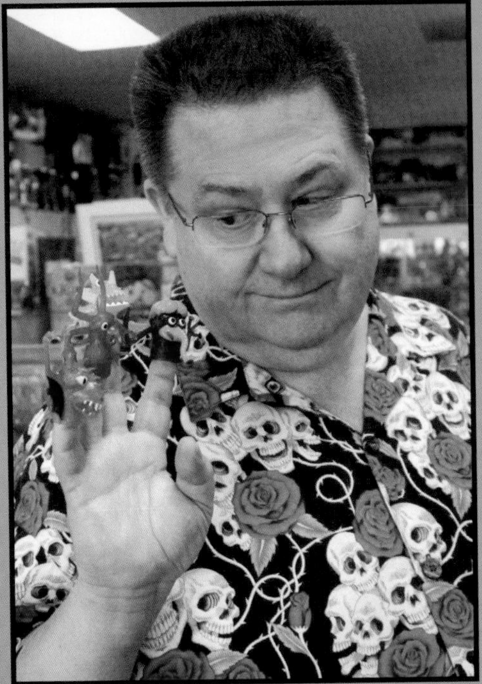

Scott Shaw! is an example of Hunter S. Thompson's statement: "When the going gets weird, the weird turn pro." An award-winning cartoonist/ writer of comicbooks, animation, advertising and toy design, Scott is also a historian of all forms of cartooning. After writing and drawing a number of underground "comix," Scott has worked on many mainstream comicbooks, including: SONIC THE HEDGEHOG (Archie); SIMPSONS COMICS, BART SIMPSON'S TREEHOUSE OF HORROR and RADIOACTIVE MAN (Bongo); WEIRD TALES OF THE RAMONES (Rhino); and his co-creation with Roy Thomas, CAPTAIN CARROT AND HIS AMAZING ZOO CREW! (DC). Scott has also worked on numerous animated cartoons, including: producing/directing of John Candy's Camp Candy (NBC/DIC/Saban) and Martin Short's The Completely Mental Misadventures of Ed Grimley (NBC/ Hanna-Barbera Productions); Garfield and Friends (CBS/Film Roman); and the Emmy-winning Jim Henson's Muppet Babies (CBS/Marvel Productions).

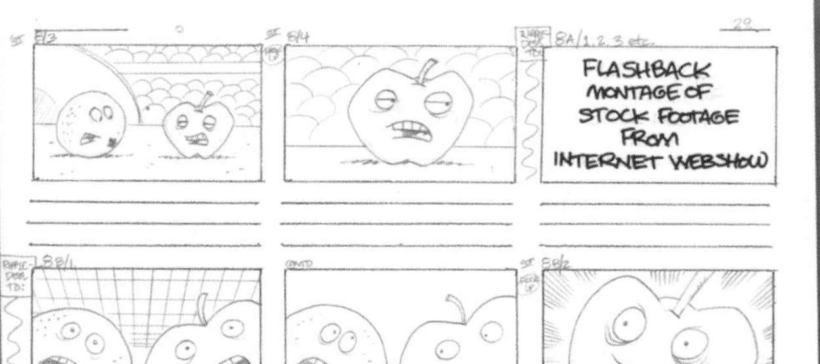
FLASHBACK
MONTAGE OF
STOCK FOOTAGE
FROM
INTERNET WEBSHOW

Above: an example of Scott's storyboards for the ANNOYING ORANGE TV series

As Senior Art Director for the Ogilvy & Mather advertising agency, Scott worked on dozens of commercials for Post Pebbles cereals with the Flintstones. He also designed a line of Hanna-Barbera action figures for McFarlane Toys. Scott was one of the comic fans who organized the first San Diego Comic-Con, where he has become known for performing his hilarious ODDBALL COMICS slide show. shawcartoons.com. Scott is also a gag man and storyboard cartoonist on Cartoon Network's ANNOYING ORANGE program. His favorite fruit is forbidden.

MIKE KAZALEH

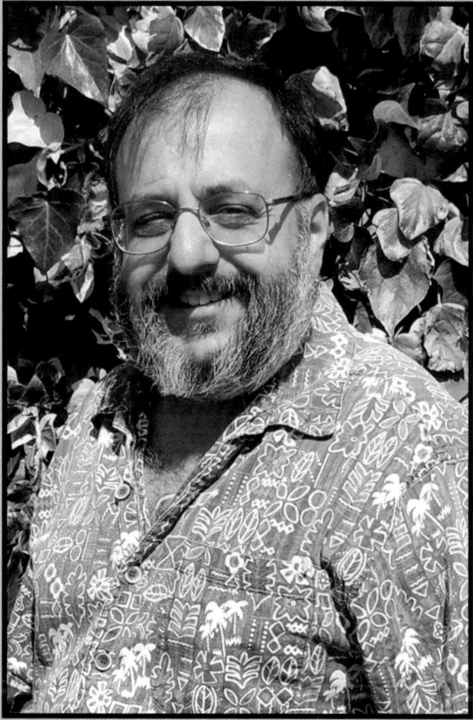

Mike Kazaleh is a veteran of comicbooks and animated cartoons. He began his career producing low budget commercials and sales films out of his tiny studio in Detroit, Michigan. Mike soon moved to Los Angeles, California and since then he has worked for most of the major cartoon studios and comicbook companies.

He has worked with such characters as The Flintstones, The Simpsons, Mighty Mouse, Krypto the Superdog, Ren and Stimpy, Cow and Chicken, and Bugs Bunny, as well as creating his own independent comics including THE ADVENTURES OF CAPTAIN JACK. Before all this stuff happened, Mike was a TV repairman.

Below: A title card designed by Mike Kazaleh.

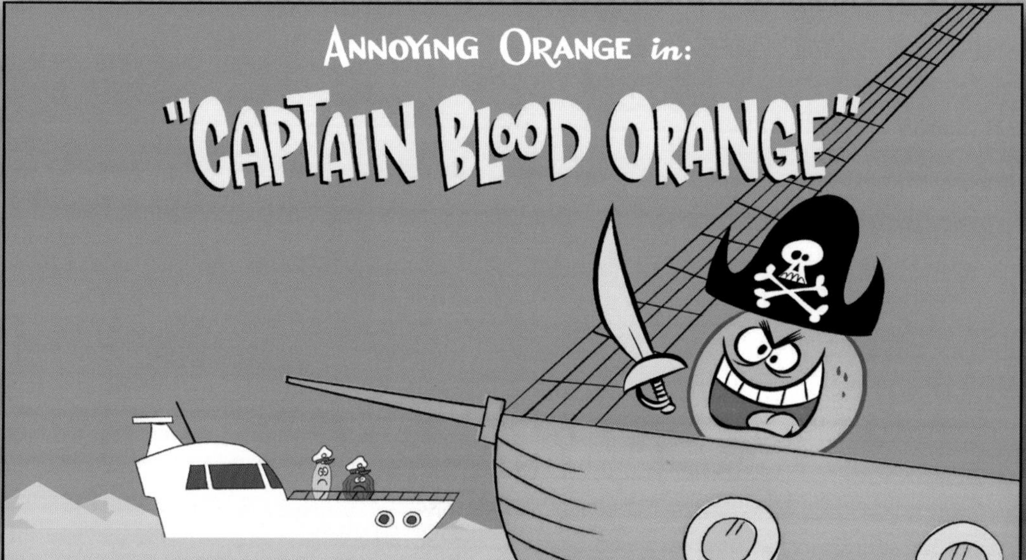
ANNOYING ORANGE in:
"CAPTAIN BLOOD ORANGE"

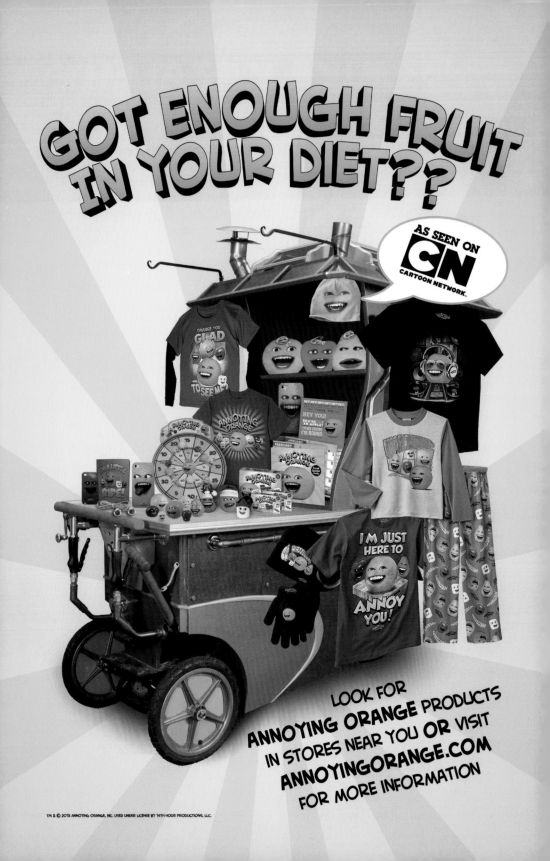

The High Fructose Adventures of Annoying Orange © 2013 14th Hour Productions. All Rights Reserved. Design © 2013 Vivendi Entertainment. 111 Universal Hollywood Drive, Suite 2260, Universal City, California 91608. CARTOON NETWORK and logo are trademarks of and © Cartoon Network. A Time Warner Company.
TM & © Annoying Orange, Inc. Used under license by 14th Hour Productions, LLC.